The Edge of War

THE
EDGE OF
WAR

Dorothy Horgan

St. Columba's High School,
Dunfermline.

Oxford University Press

Oxford Toronto Melbourne

Oxford University Press, Walton Street, Oxford OX2 6DP

Oxford New York Toronto
Delhi Bombay Calcutta Madras Karachi
Petaling Jaya Singapore Hong Kong Tokyo
Nairobi Dar es Salaam Cape Town
Melbourne Auckland

and associated companies in
Beirut Berlin Ibadan Nicosia

Oxford is a trade mark of Oxford University Press

British Library Cataloguing in Publication Data

Horgan, Dorothy
The edge of war.
I. Title
823'.914 [J]   PZ7

ISBN 0-19-271574-7

Set by Pentacor Ltd., High Wycombe, Bucks.
Printed in Great Britain by Biddles Ltd., Guildford

CHAPTER

1

'Gypsies, gypsies!' shouted a group of children, running down the steps of the Girls' Convent High School and down the path to the school gate. School had ended and they were all going home for dinner. A stone whizzed past Anna's head. She'd managed to get out of school before all the others because she knew trouble was brewing among some of the children. She ran as fast as she could to the gates, where Kati and little Nikki were waiting for her.

Anna pushed back the long, straggling, black hair out of her eyes as she ran.

'Why did they have to come?' she thought, irritated at seeing her little sister and brother. She was always telling them to go straight home, because they were in the lower school, which got out earlier than she did. 'Why do they have to tag on to me all the time? How am I supposed to become a famous singer, if I have to drag them along with me everywhere?'

That was Anna's ambition, to be a famous singer. She even had singing lessons. She used to day-dream a lot about it, and Father called her 'scatter-brains' because she'd get carried away and not notice what was really going on or what people were saying to her. But this time she'd sensed danger at school. Some girls had been whispering in groups at break and staring in her direction. When she went up to them, they stopped talking and walked away quickly, turning their backs on her to show they didn't want to have anything to do with her.

Anna grabbed the children's hands and they ran together down the cobbled street. The pavement was too narrow for all three of them to run together, even though this was the main street of the village. In fact, it was the only real street in the village, since all the others were more like paths or tracks. Anna could have run down it blindfold, she knew it so well.

'Jews, Jews!' the other children shouted, and pelted them with stones.

It was hard for little Nikki to run with the two girls, because he was only six and his legs were too short. They all kept slipping on the cobbles, which were wet with the November rain. Anna picked Nikki up and dragged Kati behind her. It was hard for Kati to run too, although she was eight, because she was short and fat, like a doughnut. Father called her 'his little Berliner', 'his little doughnut'. Her long, thick, black pigtail bobbed up and down as she ran. Anna could never be bothered with plaiting her long hair, and it just flew about in the wind.

Mother was standing with the front door open, and they all fell into the hall in a heap—Anna gasping, Kati howling, and Nikki wheezing, nearly blue in the face with trying to get his breath.

'Whatever's going on?' Mother asked, shutting the big solid door firmly, bolting it with three bolts, and locking it with a big iron key. 'Good thing I got home before you, or you'd all have been locked out there on the street.'

Mother was a teacher at the Kindergarten and usually got home first. Her dark eyes looked anxiously at the children as she pushed a strand of grey hair into the bun at the back of her neck, and stabbed it into place with a hairpin. She wasn't exactly fat, but she looked solidly built and capable. Anna felt safe with Mother in control.

'I'm never going back to that school again,' Anna said, wiping a trickle of blood from her forehead with her coat sleeve. 'Why do they call us gypsies? Why do they call us Jews? Why do they hate us?'

'Hush,' Mother said, picking up Nikki and pushing the girls in front of her through the dark hall into the kitchen at the back of the house. 'I'll have to put the steam-kettle on for Nikki,' she said. 'It's his asthma again, with all this trouble.'

She propped Nikki up on an armchair with lots of cushions, then methodically filled the steam-kettle from the tap and put it on the stove. Soon steam began to puff out and Nikki's wheezing eased up.

'They say the Jews will be taken in the night. Here in the village. That's what they're saying at school. That's what started it all off.' Anna spoke in a quiet voice, not wanting Kati and Nikki to hear.

7

'Hush,' Mother said, and she pressed her lips firmly together. 'Don't repeat anything. Walls have ears. There are secret police spying on us all the time. We're not gypsies and we're not Jews. We're Catholics, just like everybody else in this region. It's our black hair and dark eyes. Because Grandmother was Spanish.' She looked at an old-fashioned photograph of a rather grand-looking woman on the shelf above the stove. That was Mother's side of the family. Father's family were miners.

'It's not the fashion these days, black hair and dark eyes. It's dangerous to have black hair and black eyes. But all our papers are in order. And Father wouldn't be allowed to be an officer in the *Luftwaffe* if everything wasn't in order. Not these days.'

The kitchen was dark and warm because the curtain was half-drawn as usual. There was one small window over the sink, looking out on to the courtyard at the back. Just outside, by the back door, in the courtyard, was a wooden barrel with home-made sauerkraut in it. The smell of the white cabbage in the vinegar and spices used to make Anna's eyes water. But today she liked the smell of the lentil soup with sausages floating in it, which was boiling on the stove in a big black iron saucepan. It was 'Soup Day', when everybody econo-mized on food and fuel for the Fatherland, and all the meals were cooked in one pot. Sitting on a wooden stool by the stove, Anna felt happy again. Kati and Nikki were scrabbling about in the biscuit-tin, with their fear already forgotten. Here, in the kitchen of Grand-mother's house, they all felt safe.

'Anyway, I've got something to tell you.' Mother talked in a quiet voice to Anna as she put bowls of soup and sausage on the bare wooden table. 'You're thirteen now—old enough to understand these things.' She put a bowl of curd cheese on the table and some brown bread. 'We've got to move to the eastern region, to Pomerania or thereabouts. The Education Authorities are posting me to a school near a place called Stolp, near the Baltic Sea. Now don't say anything to anybody and don't ask any questions. We just have to go—no choice.' Mother was fidgeting with the plates and knives. Anna could sense her agitation. 'We've got to go at once. We'll have to pack our things tonight.'

Anna opened her mouth to ask a question, but she didn't even get it out.

'That's how it is in wartime,' Mother went on. 'Go here. Go there. No thought for anybody. We just have to make the best of it.'

So Anna didn't ask any questions. She understood why this had happened. Mother and Father weren't Party Members. If people weren't Party Members, they got sent to the worst jobs in the worst places. You just got sent and no questions asked. People who tried to be awkward got put in prison, or worse. It had happened to Uncle Hans, Mother's youngest brother. He was a medical orderly in the army, but he wasn't a Party Member, and he'd been one of the first to be sent to the eastern front. That was the worst place of all, the place that everybody was most afraid of. And Stolp was practically in Poland, about as far from Westphalia as you could get.

Anna thought she'd better change the subject. 'Will the Jews really be taken?' she asked. 'That's what they're saying in school.'

Mother closed her mouth very firmly and clearly wasn't going to say anything else on that subject.

'They say Hilda and Eva and Elspeth have all gone too,' Anna kept on.

'Gone where? What d'you mean, gone?' Mother asked in surprise, because Hilda, Eva and Elspeth were all tall, blonde, blue-eyed girls, and leaders in the Hitler Youth.

'You know—.' Anna frowned and felt embarrassed, wishing she hadn't said anything. 'Well, everybody's talking about it at school. You know—for the Fatherland. To have babies. They've volunteered for it.'

'My God,' Mother said. 'Where's it all going to end? The world's gone mad. Don't talk of these things again.' Mother turned to the other two. 'Come on and eat your dinner. After that, you can all help to pack some things.' She looked at Kati and Nikki, who were listening with interest. 'We're going away. Perhaps it won't be for long and we'll all be home for Christmas.'

'What about my singing lessons?' Anna asked. She hadn't thought of that before. Suddenly she felt anxious. Too many things were changing too fast, and she began to feel afraid without knowing why.

'I've got better things to worry about,' Mother said, and Anna knew it wasn't any use going on about it. It was no good asking Mother any more questions, because she wasn't going to answer them.

Anna sat there on her stool, looking round at the

kitchen. She didn't want to leave the old house, even though it was a bit dark and gloomy. The kitchen, with its stone-flagged floor, was warm in winter and cool in summer. The gas-mantles gave off a soft light at night, and the old stove burnt logs and all the rubbish and kept the house warm. It heated up the water as well. There was no electricity in Grandmother's house, although the schools and some of the grander houses had it.

'I won't mind saying "goodbye" to that old barrel of sauerkraut,' Anna said. 'But I don't want to leave Grandmother's house. We've always been here. We belong here.'

'It'll still be here when we get back. It's not forever, is it? And don't you worry—I'll soon get some sauerkraut going in Stolp, just to make you feel at home!' Mother was trying to make them smile, but she wasn't very successful.

Later on in the afternoon, Erika and Karl, who were friends of Mother's, came in from next door to help with the packing. Karl was big and cheerful and joked a lot, and Erika was small, with fair hair and blue eyes. They didn't have any children of their own, but they were always very kind to Anna and Kati and Nikki.

'Well,' Karl said, leaning on his crutch and shaking his right leg about. 'I can't help much here. Not since Tommy did me this favour.' He always called English soldiers 'Tommy', short for 'Tommy Atkins'. Half Karl's right leg had been shot off in the war in France, just a year ago. All that was left was a stump with a wooden stick strapped to it. Karl could get around marvellously with that leg, when he wanted to, but packing wasn't his idea of a good afternoon. So he hopped off to get a glass of beer.

Aunt Margarethe, Mother's older sister, came in too, but she sat down and drank peppermint tea and ordered her children, Maria and Kurt, to fetch and carry all the time. Maria, who was thirteen, and Kurt, who was fourteen, soon got fed up with this, and quietly disappeared out of the front door into the village.

'Well,' a man's voice suddenly boomed out. 'Have I got here at the right time? When all the work's been done?'

'Father, Father.' Anna threw her arms round her father's neck, almost knocking his peaked officer's cap off his cropped grey head. 'We didn't know you were coming.'

'Neither did I, but here I am, all the way from Cologne, just for one night. Come to keep an eye on you, little scatter-brains. You'd forget your heads if they weren't screwed on.' Father hugged them all and then he went into the front room and got a big map out of the desk drawer.

'Come on, then,' he said. 'Mother told me all about this business on the telephone. Let's see where this funny old place called Stolp is.' Father loved looking at maps, and he spread it out over the front room carpet.

'Now see here, Nikki—,' Father said. Anna thought it was like being back at school sometimes, when Father wanted to tell you something.

'Here we are,' he said, and he stubbed his finger at a point on the map near Münster. 'And here's the railway—going to here, Hanover—then to here, Berlin—then to here, Stettin—then to here, Stolp. That's a very long way, from Westphalia to the Baltic Sea. You'll have to eat and sleep on the train.'

'I don't want to go,' Nikki began to wail. Suddenly Father got angry and shouted: 'You be a good boy and help your Mother.' Nikki wailed even louder and Kati joined in.

'I don't want to go either,' she said. 'I want to stay here with my friends.' Then they started to wail together.

'For God's sake, shut those children up,' Father roared. 'Here, have some chocolate.' And he threw some pieces of chocolate on the floor. Nikki and Kati snatched them up and ran off to play upstairs in their bedroom, out of harm's way.

Anna was watching all this, but she didn't say anything. She was very proud of her father in his *Luftwaffe* officer's uniform. He was too old for flying duties, but he held the rank of officer from his service in the Great War. After that war, he hadn't gone back to the mines. He'd trained to be a teacher. Anna knew it was very unusual for the son of a miner to become an officer in the *Luftwaffe*. Nearly all the officers came from the upper class.

Father usually kept Nikki laughing with lots of funny stories, but not today. Anna could see him exchanging anxious looks with Mother. When everybody else was upstairs, Anna went into the kitchen, where she found Mother and Father talking in quiet voices, sitting at the table.

'How's it going, then?' Mother asked.

'Not good, not good,' Father said. 'Can you believe it? I've got to go for "re-education". Imagine that. It's like being back at school, sitting in silly little desks in a classroom, listening to some idiot telling us what to think.' His voice rose angrily.

'Hush,' Mother said. 'Don't let the children hear you. What's this "re-education", then?'

'For officers who aren't Party Members. Especially Catholics. Ever since the Bishop spoke out in Münster against their Euthanasia Programme, all that business about putting people down, just like dogs. Couldn't touch *him*, could they—because he's a count, the Count von Galen—one of the old aristocracy.'

'Well,' Mother said. 'They couldn't hang him. They wanted to though, didn't they? The people wouldn't have stood for that. Remember all the fuss? The whole region would've been up in arms.'

'Maybe that way would've been better. That's why they try to humiliate us all the time,' Father said. 'They insult our religion. They get at us because they can't get at him—little Nazi upstarts.'

He put on a mincing tone of voice—Father was a good mimic:

'"Now, who was that man? The man with the big Jew nose? The fool who didn't know his own name?" "Saint Paul, you mean," I shouted. "Oh, yes. Saulus-Paulus, Paulus-Saulus." They insult us like this all the time. Even the Field Marshal—Field Marshal of the *Luftwaffe*. He wears make-up. D'you know that? This is what Germany's come to.'

Suddenly Father slumped down with his head on the kitchen table.

'Take care what you say. Don't talk like this,' Mother whispered anxiously. 'No wonder you got sent for "re-education" if you've been going on like this.'

'Well, it's too late for caution now. My new posting's come through.'

'Where?' Mother asked, full of apprehension.

'The eastern front. That's where they send the "bad boys", like old Hans and me. Commandant of a Prisoner of War camp, on the eastern front.'

There was silence for a moment, and Anna came out of the shadows and put her arm round her father's neck. She could tell something was going terribly wrong. Mother was so cautious and careful that she hardly spoke to anybody outside the family, and she never went out, except to the Kindergarten or to the shops. Father was always boiling with anger and shouting a lot.

Suddenly Father straightened his back and put his thick, square hands firmly on the table. 'Listen,' he said. 'This is between the three of us. This Hitler's a maniac. Hush.' He put his hand over Mother's mouth as she was about to speak. 'Anna's old enough to know the truth. Hitler wants to press on to Moscow and Stalingrad. The fool. Napoleon failed and he'll fail too. Russia will swallow us all up in the end. If we fail at Stalingrad—and we will fail—nothing'll stop the Russians.' He turned to Anna. 'D'you know what "Stalingrad" means?'

Anna thought for a bit. 'Stalin's city?' she guessed.

'Yes—City of Steel,' Father said, and turned to Mother. 'Out there in Stolp, you won't be safe. Not when the Red Army gets on the move. It's too near the Russian frontier. When you get a message from me saying: "The steel does not melt", leave the place at once. Take the first train you can get, and come back here. Don't take anything with you—no luggage or anything. Make it look like a short visit to relatives. Buy return tickets. Get as far to the west as you can.'

Father stopped talking, because Erika and Karl had come into the kitchen.

'What's going on here? Is it a conference? Can we all join in?' Karl joked.

'We can't decide what to take and what to leave,' Mother said, smiling and trying to make everything sound quite normal, because she didn't want them to know what Father had been saying.

'Take plenty of woollies and boots. The winter's very cold in the eastern region. Take plenty to eat and drink on the train too,' Erika said. She was very practical.

'Lock up Grandmother's house and give us the key,' she went on. 'We'll keep an eye on things for you. The war'll be over by Christmas and you'll be back again. Back in time for the New Year. We'll all bring in 1942 together, like we always have—the New Year and the Feast of the Three Holy Kings.'

'Have you heard the rumour about the Jews?' Karl asked suddenly. 'Goldstein and Grauberg? Hitler's got the right way with the Jews.' He laughed heartily. 'They're all money-lenders and cheats. Killed Our Lord, didn't they?'

'Hush,' Mother said. 'Wasn't Our Lord a Jew too?'

Suddenly Anna saw a different Karl, and she felt sick, even though she didn't quite know why. Karl always seemed very friendly, but now she moved as far away from him as she could in the small kitchen.

'He's like the wolf in *Little Red Riding Hood*,' she thought.

'Goldstein and Grauberg were good Germans in 1914,' Father said, and he sounded angry again. 'In my unit in the old Flying Corps, they were. What's changed since then? Them or us?' And he spat on the kitchen floor and ground his shiny black shoe into the spittle. Anna knew Father only did that when he was very angry. Mother hated it.

'Don't do that,' she said. 'Spitting's for miners, not for officers.'

'Don't tell me what to do,' Father said. 'Anyway, I'm going to have a drink, sample my wine cellar.' He got up angrily, like a bull about to charge, and disappeared down the stone steps which led from the hallway into the wine cellar. Anna could hear him stumping down the stairs. In the cool darkness of the cellar, Father had laid up lots of bottles of wine. Nobody else was allowed in there. It was where Father went to escape, and he bolted the door on the inside. Mother sighed and turned back to the question of packing. Karl had disappeared again too.

Anna could just about remember the son of Jacob Grauberg. His name was Joseph and he'd been very good at the violin. 'Why didn't Grauberg and Goldstein leave the country when Joseph went to America?' she asked. 'I'd love to go to America. I could study singing and be famous.'

'You and your day-dreams,' Mother said. 'You don't know anything about these things. Goldstein's wife was very ill then, and when she died—well, I suppose he just lost heart. And Grauberg thought he'd be safe, I suppose, being a veteran and all that. I can't believe these things are really happening to us all.' And she went upstairs with Erika, to concentrate on the packing.

But Goldstein and Grauberg hadn't been safe. Laws had been passed against the Jews. First of all they'd had to give up their shops in the village—Goldstein was a jeweller and Grauberg made musical instruments. Then their nice houses had been taken over. Now they had to wear the yellow star of David on their ragged clothes. They weren't allowed to earn money, and when they'd sold all their valuables to buy food, there was no money left and they grew paler and thinner. They looked more like skeletons in rags than real people, Anna thought. She didn't see them any more, because they'd stopped going out of the miserable houses they'd been forced to live in. People were afraid to be seen talking to them. Everybody in the village knew they must be starving to death, and some people, like Mother and Frau Schwartz from the dairy, would leave bread and cheese and milk secretly at night, by the doors of the houses. Anna had seen the white skeletal faces peering through the ragged curtains. Then the food would disappear. But everybody was afraid of being caught. New faces in the village were probably the Gestapo, outsiders sent in to keep watch, and report people to the authorities.

When all the packing was done, Mother and Erika brought down the two suitcases and put them in the hall. Mother called out that supper was ready, and they all went into the kitchen and had apple-pancakes and peppermint tea. Mother said that peppermint tea was a good drink to have at bed-time. It was soothing and good for the nerves.

Anna wasn't surprised that Father wasn't there. When he disappeared into the cellar, it was usually for hours and hours. She noticed that Karl had turned up again, in time for supper.

Everybody talked louder than usual. They pretended to be very cheerful, and not to hear the banging and shouting and crashing coming up from the cellar.

Anna knew Father never hurt anybody when he got drunk, but he shouted a lot and threw empty wine bottles at the walls. Kati and Nikki didn't seem to notice anything, but they were very tired and were soon upstairs, fast asleep in bed, in the room they shared with Anna.

Anna could hear Father raving on, even after she'd gone to bed. The shouting sounded far-off and the crashing sounded like windows breaking in the distance. Anna could also hear Nikki wheezing and grinding his teeth. Kati was snoring. 'D'you have to grind your teeth as well?' Anna shouted at Nikki, and thumped her pillow. Nikki stopped grinding his teeth and she soon fell asleep.

CHAPTER

2

'Father's gone already. It's not fair. I wanted to say "goodbye" to him,' Anna said, full of disappointment, looking round the kitchen.

'He left before dawn,' Mother said. 'Never mind, Anna, here's the jug. The coffee's made and breakfast is on the table—and guess who drank all the milk?'

Nobody bothered to answer, because the answer was always 'Father'. He drank the milk straight from the jug. Mother had given up trying to get him to use a cup or a glass. It was no use trying to make Father more 'refined', even though he was an officer. 'Once a miner, always a miner,' he used to say.

'Go down to the dairy, Anna, and get a litre of milk and some cheese. Anybody who doesn't want bread and sausage can have bread and cheese. And don't spill the milk.' Mother gave Anna a gentle push through the door.

'I want both,' Kati said with enthusiasm.

It was still only 6.30 in the morning. Nobody was about in the dark street, and the village was veiled in an autumn mist. Anna wiped a flying cobweb from her face as she walked down the cobbled road. The dairy was only five minutes walk away, and it would be open already.

'Grüss Gott,' Frau Schwartz greeted Anna in the 'good morning' of the region. It meant 'Greet God'.

'Grüss Gott,' Anna replied, handing over the jug.

It was cool and dim in the dairy, with its stone floor and marble counter. The shop was lit by oil lamps, hanging from the ceiling. The milk stood in great metal churns in a corner by the wall. Frau Schwartz filled the jug from one of the churns with a long-handled scoop, and handed it back to Anna with another 'Grüss Gott'.

'What's that?' a loud voice shouted in the doorway. Anna jumped and backed into the shadow of the churns.

'What's that?' shouted a man in the uniform of a Gestapo officer. '"Heil Hitler" is what we say. Heil Hitler!' he shouted and raised his right hand in the Hitler salute.

'Here we always say "Grüss Gott",' Frau Schwartz muttered.

'Heil Hitler!' shouted the Gestapo officer, and hit Frau Schwartz across the face. Frau Schwartz staggered backwards and fell against the wall.

'Here we say "Grüss Gott",' she mumbled. There was blood trickling from her mouth.

'Heil Hitler, Heil Hitler, Heil Hitler!' the Gestapo officer shouted, hitting her across the face with each shout. Frau Schwartz fell in a heap on the floor behind the marble counter. Anna was hidden in the darkness

21

behind the milk-churns as the Gestapo officer turned and left.

'Take the milk and go home quickly,' a voice said. Anna came out of the shadows and saw Uncle Franz, Mother's older brother. He seemed like an old man to Anna. He was a priest in the village and he looked a very comforting figure now, a big, fat man, in his dark priest's clothes. He got up at dawn every morning, and when he'd said his morning Mass, he always went to the dairy for milk and to the bakery to get a roll.

'Hurry up,' he said. 'I'll look after Frau Schwartz.'

Anna took the jug of milk carefully and walked home by a little side road, avoiding the main street. It was lighter already, and this side path took her by some derelict houses, five in a row, but only two still had people living in them.

Suddenly she wished she'd gone by the main road as usual, because this was where the Jews lived. She kept her eyes down on the gritty path. She had to walk in the road because there wasn't any pavement here. She tried not to look up as she went past the inhabited houses, but she couldn't help it. The two front doors had been hacked down and all the windows were broken. She noticed that weeds were growing in the gutter on the roof. Clothes were scattered in the doorways and on the path, and a white nightdress was spread out like early snow on the low bushes.

Anna caught sight of something in the ditch by the roadside. She gave it a little poke with her foot. It looked like an old box. Then she realized that it was a shabby old violin case, already nearly covered by the dead leaves of the silver birch nearby. She didn't stop, but hurried on, and was glad to get home again.

'You forgot to get the cheese. Day-dreaming as usual, I suppose,' Mother said. Anna didn't want her to go on about the cheese, so she told her what happened in the dairy, and about the Jews' houses.

'So it's true then,' Mother said, wiping her hands on her apron. 'The Jews *were* taken last night. Oh, why ever didn't they leave when they could?'

'But Father said they were good Germans.' Anna was puzzled, and asked, 'Where have they gone to?'

Mother didn't answer that question. Anna noticed that there were a lot of questions she didn't answer these days. Instead she said, 'These are bad times for everybody. Don't frighten the little ones with this talk. Let's get the breakfast eaten. We've got a train to catch.' She bustled round everybody and made them hurry up. Anna knew it was no use asking that question again.

When breakfast was eaten and everything had been cleared away, Mother gave them all a paper bag each, with bread and sausage for the journey.

'I'm just going round to get Uncle Franz with his car. He'll take us all to the station. You three sit here with these two suitcases and wait till I get back.'

They all knew this was going to be quite a long wait, because Uncle Franz always went into chapel to have a good pray before he drove the car. He'd done this ever since he'd crashed into a tree on the ice last winter. So they all sat down on the suitcases.

Suddenly there was a loud knocking at the door. Anna got up and opened it. On the doorstep was the

Gestapo officer from the dairy. Anna recognized him, but he didn't recognize her because she'd been hidden in the shadows and he hadn't seen her properly.

'What's going on here? Have you got permission to travel? Show me your papers,' he shouted.

All the papers were laid out on the table, ready to be checked. Anna showed them to the officer, and he rustled through them, leaving them in an untidy heap. But Anna knew they were all in order, because Mother was always so careful.

'Not Party Members, hey? Are you in the Hitler Youth?' he demanded.

'We're all in the Catholic Youth,' Anna said nervously.

'Catholic Youth?' the man shouted, and spat. Then he looked at them all very closely, with their black hair and dark eyes. 'Bloody gypsies. The Hitler Youth wouldn't want the likes of you anyway. Where's your Swastika?'

All houses were supposed to have a Swastika Flag. It was another of the new laws. Anna knew they hadn't got one, because Father said he drew the line at that, but she pretended to look everywhere.

'I know it must be somewhere,' Anna said, and she began to count up the lies she was telling for when she went to Confession next.

'Mother washed it and ironed it only the other day. I expect she's put it in a safe place.'

The Gestapo officer began to pull out all the drawers, emptying them out on the floor. In the front room he emptied out the desk. Then he went upstairs and emptied out all the drawers in the bedrooms. No Swastika Flag.

'You'll all be in serious trouble if you don't produce a Swastika Flag,' he shouted at Anna, while he rummaged through the big mahogany wardrobe in Mother and Father's bedroom.

'Will this do?' Anna asked, holding up the flag of the old German Empire which she'd just found among Father's souvenirs of the Great War.

'If it's the best you can do, I suppose it'll have to,' the officer said, looking disgusted. 'Next time I come, you have the right flag—or else! I'll be back. Heil Hitler!'

Remembering what had happened to Frau Schwartz, Anna replied with a faint 'Heil Hitler' and a half-hearted salute.

When Mother and Uncle Franz came back, Anna told them what had happened.

'It's just as well you're going off to the eastern region,' Uncle Franz said, getting out of the car to help with the suitcases, while Mother stuffed everything back into drawers and cupboards. 'The Gestapo are like elephants—they never forget.' And he squeezed and wheezed his way back into the driving seat and took them off to the station.

The long train steamed ponderously through the seemingly endless plain, then it hurried through huddles of houses and a scramble of streets. It stopped at crowded stations and heaved out again into the countryside, until gradually darkness fell. They ate their food and closed their eyes, nodded asleep by the rhythmic swaying of the train. Outside there was total darkness, because the blackout was in force.

The train jolted to a stop and Mother prodded them all out on to an unlit platform with the suitcases. It was the middle of the night. Anna peered around her, but she couldn't see very much, partly because she was carrying Nikki, who couldn't be made to wake up, and partly because of the blackout. It wasn't much of a station, just one platform as far as she could see. Kati was almost sleep-walking, hanging on to Anna's other arm. Mother was struggling with the two suitcases.

'Can I help you?' a polite voice asked. 'Are you the family Brunner from Westphalia?'

'Thank God you're here, Father. We're quite lost,' Mother said. She called the man 'Father' because he was wearing a black suit.

The man smiled and took the suitcases. He was small and thin, with sharp blue eyes.

'Not "Father",' he said. 'You can call me Pastor Schmidt. I'm from the School Committee. We guessed you'd be on this train. You're in the eastern region now, mostly we're Protestants here.' He put the suitcases in the boot of a battered old car and they all scrambled in.

'Well,' Mother said, 'we're all Christians.'

'I hope so,' Pastor Schmidt answered quietly and drove off, with several bumps and jumps, into the unlit countryside. Anna felt her eyes closing and her head nodded forwards. She was too tired to lift it up again and fell asleep. Getting out of the car was like walking in a dream. She was too tired to think; she just followed

Mother into their new home, then the darkness of sleep swallowed her up.

Anna sat up suddenly and looked round; she was in bed—a strange bed. She rubbed the sleep out of her eyes and looked again. Things were coming back into her head. This wasn't Grandmother's house; it was the new place near Stolp. Mother appeared from behind a curtain and put her finger on her lips to warn Anna not to wake the others.

'It's like something out of *Hansel and Gretel*,' Anna whispered, looking round the room. There was half a smoked ham and three large smoked sausages hanging from the beams, and warmth came from an old iron stove with a pile of logs beside it. On the wooden table was a large oil lamp. Anna could hear Kati snoring in another corner of the room.

'Where's Nikki?' she asked.

Mother drew aside the curtain and showed her a little alcove with a bed in it for her, and a smaller bed with Nikki fast asleep in it.

'See how nice Pastor Schmidt and his wife have made it for us. There's food and wood for the stove,' Mother said. 'They've made us welcome. Good people, they are.'

'I want to explore,' Anna said, getting out of bed and testing the earthen floor with her bare foot.

'There isn't much to explore,' Mother said and smiled. 'Only a little back kitchen—no hot water. And the lavatory's in the garden.'

'Isn't there an upstairs?' Anna asked, amazed.

'No upstairs,' Mother said. 'This is enough for us.'

Anna went into the tiny kitchen, where there was only room for a large stone sink with one tap, and looked out of the window.

'Oh, Mother,' Anna said. 'It's awful. It's horrible.'

She looked at the grey sky and the flat grey landscape, and remembered the dream-like countryside of Westphalia, with its silver-birch forests and autumn mists, the castles with grass-filled moats, the old churches and the wayside altars. Anna smiled as she remembered Uncle Franz, with his left hand on the steering wheel, raising his hat every time he drove past one of these altars in his creaking old car. No wonder he hit a tree. Then Anna's smile faded.

'It's horrid here,' she said. 'All grey and bare and horrid. Look at those dreadful places—.' She pointed to the tiny farmhouses dotted on the horizon. 'Who'd want to live there? And I don't call that much of a church either,' she added, noticing Pastor Schmidt's chapel a little distance away to the left.

'Don't be silly,' Mother said sharply. 'See, we've got a little bit of land out there. We'll grow our own vegetables. Pastor Schmidt has promised to get us a goat and a kid. We'll have a few hens too. There's no shops right out here. We'll have to fend for ourselves.'

Anna was cheered up by the thought of all these animals. 'Is that the school over there?' she asked, pointing to a wooden building standing in the middle of a field, about a hundred yards away.

'That's it,' Mother laughed. 'No excuse for being late!' Anna was always in trouble for being late, because she always forgot things and had to find them at the last minute.

'It looks more like a cowshed,' Anna said grumpily.

As it turned out, the school was nothing like Anna had ever known before. Back home, all the senior girls went to the Convent High School, and all the senior boys went to the Boys' High School. Younger children went to other schools. But here there was only one class, so everybody was in it, and Mother was the only teacher. Pastor Schmidt came in sometimes and talked to the class, and Anna began to help too, with reading and writing.

Anna didn't like the children from the region at all. For a start, she could hardly understand what they were saying.

'Why don't they talk properly?' she asked.

'That's dialect. It's proper for them, isn't it?' Mother answered.

Sometimes the children from the region came to school; sometimes they didn't.

'Why don't they come every day?' Anna asked. 'They can't even read and write. And they go to sleep in the lessons,' she added scornfully.

'That's because they have to work on the farms early in the morning, and they come a long way,' Mother said. She got on with them much better than Anna and Kati and Nikki did. They kept themselves to themselves, and never played with the other children.

'Well, you don't seem to teach them very much,' Anna scoffed. 'You just show them pictures and tell them Bible stories, instead of real religion.'

'Maybe,' Mother smiled. 'I have to be very careful, a Catholic teaching in a Protestant region. Teaching religion too.' And she left it at that.

But there was one boy, older than Anna, who could read and write and speak 'proper' German, as well as the local dialect. When the boys had races to see who could run furthest, barefoot, over the stubble after the harvest had been cut, this boy always won. He wouldn't let anybody beat him, even though his feet were cut and bleeding. He was taller and thinner than the other boys, with green eyes and high cheek bones. He always wrote his name 'George K. Kempinski'. When people asked what the K stood for, he gave lots of different answers, like Konrad, Karl, Kurt, and so on. Now they'd stopped asking, which was just what he'd hoped would happen.

'What's the K really for?' Anna asked him one day.

'Wouldn't you like to know?' he snapped, and turned his back and walked off.

'That George is a very rude boy,' Anna said to Mother. 'And Kempinski is a stupid name.'

'He's a very clever boy,' Mother said. 'And some Germans in the eastern region have Polish names. They must have married each other.'

'Is that allowed?' Anna asked, surprised.

'Not now,' Mother said, and wouldn't say any more.

It had been autumn when they left Westphalia, but here winter set in hard and quick. One day they woke up and outside was snow, ice, frost, everywhere.

'Mother,' Nikki shouted. 'They've got skates. They're skating on the river.'

They all rushed to the window to look, because in the village at home in Westphalia all the skates had been collected by the Hitler Youth for the war effort. But here they could see crowds of children skating on the frozen river.

'Can we have skates again?' Nikki asked. The cold, clear air suited him and his asthma had almost disappeared.

As if in answer to his question, Pastor Schmidt and his wife appeared at the door with their arms full of skates, and they all ran off to the frozen river.

Anna left Kati and Nikki sitting in the snow, struggling with their skates, and went off round a curve in the river, keeping close to the bank. She was amazed to see somebody rolling about in the snow. She skated nearer and a boy stood up angrily. It was George.

'Why have you got your swimming things on? You'll freeze to death,' Anna said, amazed.

'Why don't you mind your own business?' he answered, putting his clothes back on and shaking the snow off his jacket. Something floated from his pocket into the snow. Anna swooped to pick it up before he did.

'That's a funny picture,' Anna said, looking at it closely. 'Is it supposed to be a picture of Our Lady? All dark and streaky like that?'

The boy put the picture carefully back in his pocket. 'It's only funny to you because you're so ignorant,' he said.

Anna didn't like being called ignorant, so she tried again. 'Has it got a name?' she asked.

'It's famous. That shows how ignorant you are,' the boy said, scornfully. 'It's Our Lady of Czestachowa—the Black Madonna—.'

Anna wasn't going to admit she'd never heard of this name, so she said: 'You don't belong to this region, do you? You're a Catholic, like us. Who are you? I won't tell.'

'What you don't know, you can't tell,' he said, but he sounded more friendly this time.

'Why did you roll in the snow?' Anna asked.

'I do it to be fit,' he said. 'To be strong. To be able to stand the cold and pain. To be strong against my enemies.'

'What enemies?' Anna asked. 'The Russians? The Americans? The English? How d'you know who your enemies are?'

'Anybody's your enemy that tries to take away your freedom. That's the main thing, freedom. I'll tell you one thing, if you like. The K stands for Kosciuszko.'

'That's an odd name,' Anna said. 'Who gave you that name? Was it your godparents?'

'No, it wasn't,' George answered. 'I gave it to myself.' And he walked off, striding grimly through the snow, not looking back.

Anna didn't know what he was talking about, but she wasn't going to shout after him, and she went back to Kati and Nikki. She wondered whether to tell Mother, but decided not to.

A few days later, when she got the chance, she asked Pastor Schmidt about the names Czestachowa and Kosciuszko. He looked surprised and rather anxious, and said that the first one was a city in Poland, and the other was the name of a great Polish patriot, a long time ago.

'I wouldn't talk too much about those names,' he warned Anna.

Suddenly Anna understood. George was really Polish. Anna knew this was a secret she could never tell anybody, because everybody knew that Hitler was going to destroy all the Poles and Russians, if he could.

CHAPTER

3

After the encounter in the snow, George was more friendly to Anna. He pointed out to her the distant farmhouse where he lived and worked in the fields. In the wooden school-house he occasionally came and sat on the same bench as Anna and Kati and Nikki. Sometimes he talked to her at break, before going off to play football with the other boys.

The long weeks of snow were followed by floods, when there was hardly any school at all. Then suddenly spring came; the floods disappeared and the fields were bright with flowers.

'You ought to get out and have a picnic,' Mother said to them one day. 'The sun's warm now and the fields have quite dried up. Why don't you go over the bridge and explore the other side of the river? But be careful. The river's still quite high.'

Kati insisted on taking the kid, using a coat-belt for a lead, as if she was walking a dog. It was easy to walk because the ground was quite flat, and they went for miles, enjoying the warmth of the sun, looking for fish in the river, and trying to catch frogs. They had their picnic and stretched out for a rest in the long grass.

'We'd better be getting back,' Anna said at last, looking at the sun dipping towards the horizon. 'It's quite a long way. We want to get back before dark.'

It was a long way. Anna had forgotten how far they'd come. Going back seemed to take longer. The sun had already turned the horizon crimson and violet before they got to the bridge. At the bridge, they stopped suddenly, not putting a foot on it. Kati picked up the kid. At the other end of the bridge, lined up like a shield-wall of primitive warriors defending their territory, were fifteen or so local children. They held pitchforks and spades in their hands, because they'd been working in the fields.

'They'll kill us,' Kati whispered in a terrified voice, hugging the kid. Nikki said nothing, but Anna saw his shoulders hunch with apprehension.

'No, they won't. Don't be so silly. They can't stop us. Come on, we've got to get home,' Anna said, sounding braver than she felt. She linked arms with the other two and marched them firmly on to the crown of the bridge. Now she could see the implacable blue eyes and red sunburnt faces of the straw-headed children blocking the other end. They looked very strong and fierce, not moving at all, just standing there, staring, with their farm-tools in their hands.

Then one boy stepped forward and shouted, 'Go home, Papists! Go home!' And he raised his hand to throw something at them. But he never threw it, because his hand was grabbed by George, who had come up behind him. Something dropped to the ground. It looked like a large potato to Anna. Then George was talking excitedly to the other children, taking no notice of the three on the bridge. He waved his arms about and pointed to a bare patch at the edge of the field, and then he led the children off to the hedge, which bordered the field, and they all began to drag dead wood and leaves to the bare patch, rapidly making a large pile. Then they stuffed potatoes in at the bottom, and lit the bonfire. At first it was very smoky, and they began to poke it with their forks and spades, laughing and dodging the smoke and the red sparks.

'Are they going to put us on the bonfire?' Kati asked fearfully. 'They're not going to get my little pet.' She hugged the kid even tighter, and it let out a bleat of complaint.

The three children sat down on the crown of the bridge, not knowing what to make of the bonfire. Anna was wondering what to do. The other children seemed to be playing round the bonfire just like they them-selves used to play round bonfires, back in Westphalia. Had she been wrong about them? Perhaps they weren't so different after all.

'They're just having a bonfire,' she snapped, sud-denly feeling tired and irritated by Kati's fearfulness.

Then the bonfire got going properly and the children began to dance round it, clapping their hands in time with the steps, and singing a song Anna didn't know. A strange, sad song, it sounded, reminding Anna of the cries of sea-birds.

George left the dancing children and came up to the

three on the bridge. 'Come on,' he said. 'Join in. We're roasting potatoes in the bonfire and they'll be ready soon. There's enough for you.'

'Will they let us?' Anna asked nervously.

'Of course they will,' George said. 'If you weren't so snooty to them, they'd be nicer to you. Can't you see you frighten them? So haughty and posh. You won't even try to talk to them. What d'you expect?'

Anna was surprised at what George had said. She hadn't thought of it like that.

'Well, come on,' George said, pulling Anna's hand. Anna grabbed Kati's hand, and Kati grabbed Nikki's, and they ran in a line to the other side of the bridge, with the kid trotting behind on the lead.

The children dancing and singing round the bonfire didn't stop for them: George opened up a gap in the circle and they joined in.

Then the circle of dancers broke up, and some of them sat down round the fire, while a group of boys did a wild folk dance that Anna had never seen before. She joined in with the others, clapping in time with the dance. Some of the children crowded round Kati and Nikki, wanting to stroke the kid and feed it with leaves. One of the boys poked the bonfire with his pitchfork and the flames and sparks flew up in the air. They began to sing folk songs, and Anna joined in the ones that she knew. When the children found out that Anna knew lots of folk songs, they shouted to her to sing some more. So Anna sang, and they clapped to the beat and joined in the choruses.

Then the boys dragged the charred potatoes from the

red-grey ashes with their forks, and shared them out.
The kid enjoyed them, and tried to eat up all the burnt
skins. Anna didn't care much for the smoky taste, but
she pretended to enjoy it. Kati and Nikki were asking
for more, trying to talk to the children in the local
dialect. This made them all laugh a lot.

'See, if they can do it, you can,' George said, nodding
in the direction of Kati and Nikki, who were chattering
away. They all laughed when Nikki blacked his face
with a charred potato skin.

'We'll have to go,' Anna said, seeing the evening star
above the horizon and realizing how dark it was.

'We'll have to go, too,' the others said, and they
banged the fire out with their spades, sending sparks in
all directions. Then they covered the hot ashes with
soil, until it was all black and cold and damp.

Suddenly it was quite dark, and Anna made Kati and
Nikki run all the way home, while they shouted
goodbye and waved to the others, who were scattering
in all directions until they were hidden in the darkness.

'Whatever have you been doing?' Mother gasped,
looking at Nikki's blackened face, and three pairs of
very dirty hands, and they told her the whole story
while she boiled up some water for them to wash in.

The summer months were very hot and bright, and
the school was half-empty, because the children were
working in the fields. Anna and Kati and Nikki went
swimming in the river almost every day, and Kati and
Nikki made lots of new friends. Anna still found it
difficult to talk to the local children, but at least she had
George to talk to.

Looking in the mirror propped up behind the tap in the kitchen, Anna saw how dark-skinned she'd got with the sun. 'I really do look a bit Spanish,' she thought. 'And so do Kati and Nikki. We don't look a bit like the people who belong here.'

'What are you thinking about?' Mother asked, coming into the kitchen. When she heard what Anna had to say, she smiled. 'It's the inside that counts, not the outside,' she said. 'Colour doesn't make a person better or worse. You've got to look a bit deeper than that.'

But summer was brief in Stolp. The lengthening nights gradually overtook the sunny days. One morning Anna woke up with a shiver and looked out of the window to see the grey, cold mist rolling off the river. Summer had ended. It was winter again.

CHAPTER

4

'It's like being in the middle of nowhere, here,' Anna said, looking out at the acres of snow and ice. 'I mean, you wouldn't think there was a war on, or anything. Nothing ever happens here.'

'Maybe you should be glad of that,' Mother said sharply. 'Day-dreaming again. That's you all over. Poor Uncle Hans reported missing, and no word from Father for over a year. And I don't like the sound of what I've heard on Pastor Schmidt's wireless.'

Mother gave the hen-food a good stir. 'Make yourself useful and feed the hens,' she said.

'Let me do it!' Kati shouted. 'Last time Anna did it, she forgot to lock the door afterwards. We had to chase them all over the place. And her stocking's fallen down again.'

'Oh, Anna!' Mother said, looking at the black woollen stocking coiled round Anna's right ankle. 'Where's your garter? Can't you look after yourself better than that?'

'It was too tight, so I took it off. Now it's lost.' Anna sounded as if she couldn't care less.

'I don't know what I'm going to do about you, Anna,'
Mother said, with a sigh. 'Anyway, Pastor Schmidt and
his wife are giving me a lift into town. I can do some
Christmas shopping. Try to keep an eye on things,
Anna. And find another garter.'

Mother went out, all muffled up against the bitter
cold. There had been no school for over a week, because
of the snowfall. The children from the isolated farms
were cut off. Only the main road to Stolp was still open.

'I suppose that means another Christmas with the
Schmidts, being all polite and no second helpings,' Kati
said, pulling a face and remembering the first Christmas
away from their home in Westphalia. It hadn't been
very cheerful.

'All you ever think of is food,' Nikki said. 'I like
Pastor Schmidt. He showed me how the car engine
works.' Nikki was getting quite strong and healthy.

'Well, it's all right for you two,' Anna said. 'All you
want to do is play. It's boring for me. Boring, boring,
boring.'

'Just because school's closed and you can't see
George Kempinski,' Kati jeered.

'Shut up!' Anna said furiously, and threw a handful
of hen-food at Kati. But George was the only friend she
had out here. Without him to talk to there was only Kati
and Nikki, who were still babies in her opinion.

When Mother came back from the shopping trip, Kati
and Nikki were too busy unloading her bags to notice
the expression on her face. 'There's a card from Father,'
she said to Anna.

Anna couldn't understand why Mother didn't sound

really pleased. She looked at the card. There was 'Happy Christmas' written on one side, and on the other, a very short message: 'The steel does not melt. Love, Father.'

'The clerk in the post office gave me a very funny look when he handed over the card,' Mother said. 'They read everything. I said it was to help you with your chemistry homework. You can't be too careful. There are informers everywhere. Anyway, I've made all the arrangements. We've got to do exactly what Father said; he knows what he's talking about. Pastor Schmidt will see to the animals. I've asked him already. And he'll give us a lift to the station tomorrow. I told him we're going to Grandmother's house for Christmas. And that's all I've told him. He'll have to report to the School Committee when I don't turn up and the house is empty. We don't want him to get into any sort of trouble.'

'Do we have to go straightaway?' Anna asked. 'As quick as that?'

'You know what Father said. At once. Buy return tickets and don't take any luggage. That's what he said. We'll have to keep quiet about it, or we'll end up in prison, or worse.'

Kati and Nikki had got into the conversation.

'But what about my skates?' Nikki asked. 'I can't leave my skates. I've got to take them.'

'No skates,' Mother said, and she meant it. 'You'd be the only child in the village with skates. That would look very odd.'

'I want to take the goats and hens with me,' Kati moaned.

'No animals,' Mother said. 'Just something to eat on the train, and that's all. No arguments.'

The next day, they locked up the house, gave the key to Pastor Schmidt, and left Stolp as suddenly as they'd come.

'Don't stare. It's rude to stare,' Mother said in a loud whisper.

The train had pulled up in Berlin. They were all crowded on top of each other, Nikki on Mother's knee and Kati on Anna's. The train was packed with servicemen. Anna had never seen so many men in uniforms before, all carrying kitbags, crammed together in the corridors.

'Look out of the other window,' Mother was whispering.

'But I can't help looking,' Nikki said. 'Are all those soldiers dead?'

'No, of course not. They're wounded. From the eastern front,' Mother answered.

One platform was completely covered with the wounded, some lying on stretchers, some just lying on the floor of the platform. Heads, faces, arms, and legs were covered in blood-stained bandages.

'They'll die of cold,' Anna said. 'Why don't they cover them up?'

'They're coming through by the hundred,' one of the

passengers said. 'Can't move them quick enough. Well, I suppose the war's over for them, poor devils.'

'They're the lucky ones, if you ask me,' another passenger muttered.

The other people in the carriage went quiet when he said that, and tried to edge further away from him, as if they were afraid of being too close to him, but it was too crowded. Nobody said anything for a long time. The journey was very slow and uncomfortable. There was no heating, so they all huddled together to keep warm. The train kept stopping even where there was no station. At Hanover they stopped for a long time because there was an air-raid in progress. Anna peered through the blackout blinds and saw that the sky was criss-crossed with searchlights and lit in sudden bursts of exploding shells. The journey seemed to take forever, but at last they were home, cold and tired and hungry.

Erika and Karl were amazed to see them all standing on their doorstep.

'We've called for the key,' Mother said, very tired. The walk from the station had been almost too much for them, even though they hadn't got any luggage to carry.

'You poor things. You're all worn out. You never let us know you were coming home for Christmas. We'd have met you at the station and got the house warmed up. Now it'll be like old times again,' Erika said, full of delight.

They soon settled down to the old routine in Grandmother's house. Very soon Mother got a barrel of sauerkraut pickling by the back door again. When letters came from the School Committee in Stolp, she just burnt them and pretended they'd heard nothing. Lots of letters got lost, when the mail trains got bombed.

Kati insisted on keeping hens again, and even raked over part of the courtyard to plant potatoes.

'No goats,' Mother said. 'I draw the line at having smelly goats on the back doorstep.' Anna privately thought that the sauerkraut was just as smelly as the goats.

Christmas was a great success, followed by the New Year and the Feast of the Three Holy Kings. Karl and Erika joined the family in Grandmother's house and there was plenty to eat and drink.

'It's more fun here,' Nikki said. 'We didn't get all these feast days in the eastern region. I like it better here.' And everybody agreed with him.

'It would be even better if Father was here,' Kati said, and everybody agreed with that too. But there had been no more news from him for a long time.

'I suppose that's how it is in wartime,' Mother said, and she sounded tired. 'You've just got to hope for the best.'

'Do we have to go back to school after the Christmas holiday?' Kati asked. 'Back to our old school? Couldn't we just stay at home?'

But back to school it was after Christmas, and Anna thought it was almost as if they'd never been away, except when she thought about George. But they didn't talk much to the other children about their stay in the eastern region. They even got used to the air-raid warnings at night. The RAF never bothered to drop bombs on the village; they were usually looking for the Dortmund-Ems Canal and the heavy industries of the Ruhr. So on the whole the people in the village didn't take much notice of the air-raid warnings. They just stayed in bed.

One day, early in March, Anna came running home from school. 'Mother, Mother,' she shouted, banging on the front door.

'Whatever's the matter?' Mother asked, holding the door open.

'They've taken Uncle Franz. The Gestapo. They came into the school.'

'Whatever d'you mean?' Mother couldn't believe what she was hearing.

'It's true,' Anna gasped, sitting down on a stool in the kitchen. 'They've taken Uncle Franz and Father Wilhelm and another Father. They were all in school. To give us religious instruction. For Lent. And the Gestapo just came in and took them all off in a van. The Sisters are all going mad.'

'Quick, Anna,' Mother said. 'Go and get Aunt Margarethe and Karl and Erika. We'll have to do something quickly, before Franz disappears entirely. That's what happens these days—people just disappear.'

'Like Grauberg and Goldstein did?' Anna asked.

'Nobody's safe these days,' Mother said, shaking her head.

'Well,' Karl said, when they were all sitting round the kitchen table, 'what can we do? We don't even know where they've been taken. We'll have to be very careful, or it'll be our turn next.'

'I've decided what I'm going to do,' Mother said. 'I'm going to Münster to see the Bishop, the Count von Galen. He's our best chance. They can't touch him, and he'll know what to do. I'll go tomorrow. We mustn't waste any time. I'll stay in Münster until I find something out. Erika and Margarethe, you'll keep an eye on the children for me, won't you?'

'No problem,' they both said, when they saw her mind was really made up. Kati and Nikki didn't look too pleased about it, but nobody was going to take any notice of them, so they didn't say anything.

'I'll come to the station with you, and see you off,' Anna said to Mother, early the next morning. The station was a good walk from Grandmother's house, a little outside the village, and all the way Mother was giving Anna instructions.

'Don't be late for school'—'Don't let Kati and Nikki be late for school'—'Don't forget to feed the hens'—'Don't forget to put on clean clothes'—and so on. She was still giving instructions when she got on the train and her words were drowned in the noise from the steam-engine. Anna waved goodbye.

On the way home Anna was trying to remember all the instructions.

'I'll never manage to do all those things—not at the right time and in the right order,' she thought. Then she was distracted from these worries by loud shouting on the other side of the high hedge that grew along the roadside. Behind the hedge were fields where crops were being planted. Although Anna couldn't see over the top of the hedge, she could see through it easily because there weren't any leaves on it, and she was amazed to see soldiers with guns and whips in their hands, shouting at the men working in the field and hitting them with the whips. She'd heard that foreign labourers had been brought in, but she'd thought it would be like it had been in Stolp, where everybody worked on the land. There hadn't been guns and whips there.

Now one of the workers had fallen down and a soldier was standing over him, shouting and hitting him. When another worker came to help him, he was knocked down too. The workers were so thin and ragged that Anna thought they looked like rows of scarecrows swaying in the wind. Then she heard a car coming down the road, so she jumped away from the hedge and walked quickly home, acting as if she hadn't seen anything.

When Anna got back home, she wondered what she ought to do, but there was nobody to ask. Perhaps she shouldn't do anything? But then she remembered how Mother had taken food secretly at night to the Jews' houses, before they had been taken away. Anna decided to do the same, but without telling anybody, because Kati and Nikki were too young, and because she had never really trusted Karl after he'd said that Hitler had the right way with the Jews. And that meant she couldn't tell Erika either, and Aunt Margarethe was too old and set in her ways.

That night, after Kati and Nikki had gone asleep,

Anna went out with some bread and pieces of sausage in a basket. If anybody stopped her, she was going to say that she was gathering mushrooms, because that was what quite a lot of people did in the very early morning.

It was all quiet along the dark road and nobody bothered her. She put the food down at intervals under the hedge and went home. All was peaceful.

The next afternoon she walked along the road and, without actually stopping, looked under the hedge. The food had gone. She decided to go again with more food that night.

Anna set off again. The night was bright and clear, with a full moon. It was almost like daylight. As soon as she got closer to the hedge, Anna was surprised to hear noises on the other side of it, shouting and loud voices. She crouched close by the hedge, afraid to move. Then she guessed what had happened. The labourers were working at night, as well as by day, because the moon was so bright.

Anna quickly put down all the food where she was crouching, making the sign of the cross on the bottom of the last loaf she put down. That surprised her. Why ever had she done that? That was what Mother and Father did, before they cut into a new loaf. Anna was always embarrassed by it, and thought it was the sort of thing peasants did, always crossing themselves and everything else in sight.

As all these thoughts were rushing through her mind, she caught sight of one of the slave-workers. He put his finger on his lips, warning her to be quiet. As the moonlight fell on his face, Anna very briefly saw his high cheek bones and green eyes. Then a guard came up behind him, shouting and waving his gun. Anna ran for her life, out of sight, round the corner, and all the way back to Grandmother's house.

As she lay in bed, shaking and gasping for breath, thoughts rushed through her head. Could it really be George? He looked too thin. But all the slave-workers were thin. How strange that he should be here, if it was him. If it was George, who had betrayed him? Who had guessed his secret, besides her? Would he think *she* had betrayed him? Had the guard seen her? Would they come for her? Finally, she fell into a sleep full of nightmares, and she was glad to wake up as soon as the dawn came.

Nobody came for Anna. Later that week, there was a letter from Mother. It said that the Bishop had found out where Uncle Franz had been taken by the Gestapo. It was to a labour camp near Munich, in the south of Germany, to a little village called Dachau. Mother asked Aunt Margarethe to send some money to her at the hotel in Münster, because she was determined to go to Dachau and visit Uncle Franz, taking food and clothes for him.

Aunt Margarethe sent the money straightaway, and they waited to get another letter from Mother saying she'd received the money. No letter came. Days went by. Then a week. Then two weeks.

Then one afternoon Aunt Margarethe came round to Grandmother's house with a letter in her hand.

'Is it from Mother?' Anna asked eagerly, and Kati and Nikki came running up.

Aunt Margarethe looked at them. Anna could see something was very wrong.

'What's the matter?' she asked.

Without a word, Aunt Margarethe handed her the letter. It was from the main post office in Münster. It contained a brief note and the letter which Aunt Margarethe had sent to Mother, returned unopened. The note said: 'This hotel was destroyed by enemy action. No survivors.'

It took days before this news really sank in, and it was only the efforts of Aunt Margarethe and Erika that kept things going. Anna didn't know how they were going to manage without Mother. Kati and Nikki had been late for school three times in one week, and Anna had been late every day. Kati took over the job of feeding the hens, because Anna tried putting sauerkraut in the hen-food and nearly poisoned them. Anna could never remember about clean clothes or washing their hair. Aunt Margarethe and Erika kept the house in order and got them all cleaned up for school two or three times a week.

One day Aunt Margarethe took Anna out to pick mushrooms. They went along the road where the slave-workers were. There were armed guards by the roadside, and wooden towers had been put up with armed guards on the look-out. Anna knew she'd never be able to put food by the hedge again. What would happen to George? Was it really George she'd seen? Perhaps she'd never know the answers to these questions.

Nikki and Kati cried a lot and kept looking out of the window. They couldn't believe that Mother wasn't going to come home again. They wet the beds at night and Erika and Aunt Margarethe sighed a lot and took away armfuls of washing.

Spring turned into summer, then autumn followed and the long cold winter. Kati and Nikki often ended up in Anna's bed, so she pushed it against the wall so that they wouldn't fall out.

Aunt Margarethe and Erika took it in turns to bring round hot meals in big cardboard boxes, until one day the gravy and the sauerkraut spilt on the bottom of the box. The cardboard gave way, and the dinner ended up on the road, with a stray dog lapping it all up. Then Aunt Margarethe said enough was enough. Anna would have to learn how to cook, and she was going to teach her.

It took Anna a long time to learn, but as the weeks and months went by, and another Christmas came and went, Grandmother's house got more organized again, and Kati and Nikki began to settle down a little. Aunt Margarethe arranged for Anna to start her singing lessons again, to take her mind off things. Summer came round again with at least the appearance of normality.

CHAPTER

5

One Sunday evening, in the autumn of 1944, without any warning, Uncle Hans turned up on the doorstep— Uncle Hans who'd been sent to the eastern front as a medical orderly and been reported missing two years ago.

Anna heard a knock on the door and went to open it. At first she didn't recognize him at all: she saw a man as bony as a skeleton. His grey field-coat seemed to be holding him up. His eyes were staring and large, and his cheeks were so thin that his jaws and teeth stuck out, like a skull in a museum.

He held his arms out to Anna, but when he tried to speak, his lips stuck to his teeth.

'Is it really you, Uncle Hans?' Anna whispered, pulling him into the house. Kati and Nikki peered at him fearfully as he came and sat in the kitchen. He looked round without saying anything, and Anna put some milk and water on to boil and cut a slice of bread and cheese.

'Can you eat that?' she asked.

Uncle Hans managed a real smile. He dipped the bread in the hot milk and let the cheese make greasy rings in it. Then he gobbled it up like a starving man.

'Where's Mother?' he asked at last.

Anna told him. It didn't seem like more than a year ago that Mother had left for Münster; it seemed either like yesterday or forever. It seemed like yesterday that she'd said goodbye to Mother at the station; but it seemed like forever that she'd been cold and tired, dreaming every night that Mother and Father had come back home again. Every morning she woke up and tried to make the dream last longer, but Nikki always woke up crying and Kati always woke up hungry, so Anna had to get up and look after them.

Uncle Hans sat without speaking for a while, sitting there looking into some vague distance. Then he said: 'I've got news of your father. Not good news, I'm afraid. Court-martialled, he was. That was back in '43. All in secret. Everything's in secret these days. I heard it on the grapevine. That's how news spreads out in the east. Nobody knows where the news comes from, but everybody spreads it. Two hundred of his Russkie POWs escaped—can you believe it? Two hundred. Well, he was the Commandant. Let 'em go, that's what they say. Turned a blind eye. Treated worse than animals, they were; a handful of food each day and forced labour. Your father couldn't stand it—let 'em go. Court-martialled. Saved from the firing-squad by his friend, a doctor. Pleaded insanity—nervous breakdown. Then he got sent to a military hospital—loony-bin, really. Makes you wonder who the real loonies are.'

'But where, where?' Anna asked, hope lighting up her face.

'Cologne,' Uncle Hans answered.

Anna's heart sank and the hope faded.

'But there's nothing left of Cologne, hardly,' she said. 'It's all bombed to bits.'

'That's right. 'fraid so,' Uncle Hans said, and sank into silence again.

After a while, Anna couldn't bear the silence any longer, but she didn't dare to ask any more questions about Father. She wanted to hope he was still alive.

'What happened to you, Uncle Hans?' she asked at last.

'Taken prisoner, I was. By the Russkies. Funny old world, isn't it? Not a bad lot, at the front. We're all just soldiers there. The further away from the front, the worse it gets. All politicians, back there where it's safe. They were going to ship us back into Russia, and a guard tips me the wink. I slipped off the wagon one night; very foggy, it was. I've walked, run, swam, crawled, got lifts—you name it, I've done it. It's chaos out there in the east. Roads full of refugees running from the Russkies. Only a matter of time before Hitler's rotten ship goes down. Wants to take us all down with him. I'm not fighting his bloody war any more.'

'We'll hide you,' Anna said. 'In the cellar, with Father's wine! If the SS find you, they'll shoot you straight off for a deserter. But hardly anybody from the outside comes to the village now. We'll make it look like you're wounded. There's lots of wounded, back from the front, even in the village.'

Anna gave Kati an old sheet to tear into strips, and Nikki helped.

'I know,' Anna said, looking more cheerful, 'we'll have one of the chickens tonight. We'll have a secret welcome-home party for Uncle Hans. Just us three, and Erika and Karl, and Aunt Margarethe and Maria. It's a pity Kurt's been called up. He could have come too. Then we'll put chicken's blood on the bandages—that'll make it look more convincing.'

Anna went off to get Karl to wring the chicken's neck and cut off its head, which he did, in spite of Kati's shrieks and shouts. Then Anna went round to tell Aunt Margarethe the news about Uncle Hans.

When she got back to Grandmother's house, Uncle Hans had fallen asleep in a chair. Anna spattered chicken's blood on the homemade bandages, and with the help of Kati and Nikki, she bandaged up his arms and legs, and even his head, remembering what the wounded had looked like on the station platform in Berlin. Uncle Hans hardly bothered to wake up while all this was going on, but in the end, when he managed to open his eyes properly, he was very surprised to see what he looked like.

'You've done a good job there,' he said to Anna. 'I'm beginning to feel quite sorry for myself! Can't be too careful. I'll stay in the cellar, out of sight. Won't be short of a glass of wine down there, will I?'

That evening they had a good dinner to welcome Uncle Hans back. When Karl heard the story about Father, he went to telephone Cologne, to get some information about the hospital and the patients. When he came back, he shook his head.

'Bombed out,' he said. 'Most of the hospital records destroyed. But—and don't get too hopeful—some of the patients, the walking wounded, had been evacuated to Holy Cross Hospital, out in the country. But I couldn't find out any names. Best I could do, I'm afraid.'

'But Father might be alive, mightn't he?' Anna said eagerly.

'Don't get too hopeful. There are lots of things that might have happened—mostly bad,' Karl said, not wanting to raise Anna's hopes.

'But we'll have to find out. Go to Holy Cross. I know how to get there. That's where Kati had her tonsils out. It's only a short ride on the bus outside Münster,' Anna said.

'And who d'you think's going to go to Münster? There's raids all the time. It's not safe,' Erika said.

'I can't go. Not with the old wooden leg,' Karl said.

'Uncle Hans can't go either, and nobody knows where Kurt is,' Anna said. 'We've got to keep Uncle Hans hidden.'

'Well, got to look after Number One, these days,' Karl said. 'No point in looking for trouble. That's where your father went wrong.'

'I'll go myself,' Anna said firmly. 'I've been before and I know the way.'

'That's crazy,' Erika said sharply. 'All these air-raids. Any minute now the English and the Americans will be invading us. They're right on our doorstep already. You should stay here. At least it's a bit safer here. Nobody's going to bother with our little village.'

But Anna was quite determined to set off the next day, and nothing anybody said was going to stop her.

Very early the next morning Anna set off for the station, with some sandwiches in a paper bag, leaving Uncle Hans in charge of Kati and Nikki. She had to go past the fields where the foreign slave-workers were already working. She wondered about George, but there was no chance of stopping, now that armed guards were everywhere and the look-out towers had been built.

Anna stood and waited a very long time on the railway platform. Because of the air-raids, trains were now very infrequent and didn't run to a set timetable any more. Anna decided that if a train didn't come by midday, she'd go home and try again tomorrow. But she was lucky. A train came, but it was so crowded that Anna had to squeeze in as best she could, clambering up on to the luggage-rack. A lot of people were hanging on to the outside of the carriages, and every time the train stopped, even more people pushed in and hung on.

When Anna got to Münster, she had to scramble over piles of bricks and stones, and walk in the middle of the road, because of the danger of falling buildings. The air smelt of burning rubble and made her throat sore. But the roads round the bus station had been cleared and Anna squeezed into the country bus between two large farm-women who had been in the town selling food from their farms.

The bus put Anna down at the end of a country lane. She knew where she was. This lane led through the trees to Holy Cross Hospital. It was all quiet and peaceful; the autumn sun was shining, and the war seemed a long way off. Anna walked cheerfully along, eating her sandwiches. A young dog came bounding out of the trees and stood in front of her, wagging its tail and looking hungrily at her food.

'Here you are, dog,' Anna said, and threw a crust to the dog. It swallowed it in one gulp and looked eagerly for more.

'Sorry,' Anna laughed. 'All gone. Here, catch this.' She screwed up the paper bag into a ball and threw it down the lane. The dog gave a woof of joy and bounded after it. It brought back the paper ball in its mouth and laid it at Anna's feet.

'You want to play, don't you?' Anna said. The dog flattened its ears and nuzzled her ankles. Its tail never stopped wagging.

'Come on, then.' Anna threw the paper ball again. Back came the dog and dropped the ball at her feet. They kept the game up until Anna was right outside the huge main doors of the hospital.

'Sorry, dog,' Anna said. 'Sit. Wait if you want. You can't come in here.'

The dog sat obediently by the door, guarding the paper ball, its tail still pounding on the ground.

Anna walked carefully on the vast polished floor,

past a row of potted palms, past a huge tank of tropical fish, to a great shining reception desk in carved walnut.

'It's like being in a cathedral,' Anna thought. 'I wonder why everybody's so quiet, not even talking to each other.'

It was true. The people who were sitting in comfortable armchairs, reading magazines, didn't even look up as she went by.

'Yes?' asked the receptionist, who didn't want her time wasted by a girl who ought to be at school.

'I wish to enquire about my father,' Anna said firmly. 'He's an officer in the *Luftwaffe*. His name is Brunner.'

At the mention of the word 'officer', the receptionist became noticeably more polite. She pulled open a huge drawer in the desk. Anna could see two files, one black and one red. The receptionist took out the black file and closed the drawer quickly, as if she didn't want Anna looking inside it. She ran her finger down the list of names beginning with B.

'I'm sorry,' she said. 'There's no Brunner here. You must be mistaken.'

'What about the other file? Why don't you look in there?' Anna asked, thinking she'd come too far to go away with no news at all.

'There is no other file,' the receptionist snapped. 'Please leave now. You're wasting my time.'

Anna could tell by the tone of the receptionist's voice that she'd better go quickly, so she left. Outside the main doors she sat and played with her new friend, the young springer spaniel.

'Why did the receptionist lie?' she wondered. 'There

was another file. A red one. I saw it. She doesn't want me to see it, that's what it is. I bet there's more names in the red file—people like Father, who've been court-martialled or something. Red for danger. I bet that's what it is.'

Anna was talking to the dog and scratching behind its ears. The dog liked this and nuzzled for more attention. Anna had an idea.

'Would you like to help me?' she asked the dog. 'Would you like a nice game in there?' She nodded towards the hospital. The dog jumped up and woofed and wagged its tail.

'Come on, then,' Anna said, screwing the soggy paper bag into a ball again. She opened the big doors and threw the ball along the polished floor. The springer followed it, its legs going in all directions as its paws slid helplessly on the slippery surface. First the dog hit one of the potted palms. Down it went with a crash that made all the people look up in alarm. The receptionist looked up in time to see the dog taking a playful leap at the fish tank. She let out a scream and began to chase the dog. The dog thought this was all part of the game and leapt over the fish tank, landed on the other side, and sent a vase of flowers all over the floor. By this time, several people had joined in, trying to catch the springer, but the dog only got more and more excited and determined not to get caught. It was the best game it had had for ages. It leapt, slid, woofed, skidded. Chairs and tables went over, and people fell over each other as they tried to catch the dog.

While the dog and the people chasing it were all

getting tangled up in potted palms and floral decor-
ations, Anna ran quickly to the desk. Crouching out of
sight behind it, she pulled open the big drawer and
opened the red file. On the first page, in big letters, she
read:

ATTENTION TO ALL NURSING STAFF

These patients are dangerous prisoners and enemies
of the Fatherland. Total security and a blackout of all
information must be maintained at all times.

Anna flipped over two pages. Names beginning with B
were always easy to find, always at the front of any list.
There it was:

BRUNNER, N – WARD K.12

'Just what d'you think you're doing?'
Anna looked up to see the angry receptionist.
'Take that dog and get out of here before I call the
police,' she shouted.
The dog had already come panting up to Anna with
the wet paper ball in its mouth. It wagged its tail
furiously, hoping for more fun.
Anna got to the door as quickly as she could,
stepping over the broken vases, flowers, palm trees,
and tipped-over chairs and tables. The dog went
bounding ahead of her, crashing into the big doors,

leaving scratch-marks on the polished wood with its eager paws.

Once outside again, Anna was satisfied. That was Father's name. He was alive and he was there. They wouldn't put a ward number by the name of a person who was dead. Anna threw the soggy paper ball into the trees and the dog ran after it. Before it came back, Anna was on the return bus. From the window she could see the dog hopefully wagging its tail at the bus stop, with the paper ball at its feet. Then it bounded out of sight into the trees again.

CHAPTER

6

Getting home was going to be a great rush. Anna knew she'd have to get a train before nightfall, because of the heavy night raids on the railways. The sky would be lit up by searchlights, tracer bullets, exploding shells and the red flares dropped by the RAF. Anna hurried off the bus, and ran, scrambled and stumbled over the rubble left by the air-raids, taking as many short cuts as she knew. In the distance, she could hear the train whistle. She got to the station, quite out of breath, showed her pass to the guard, and ran after the train. It was already on the move, pulling away from the platform. The guard leaned out of the guard's van at the very end of the train, and waved her on. She ran with her hands out, and he grabbed them, and hauled her aboard. She lay on the floor of the guard's van, gasping for breath. The guard gave her a friendly nod.

'Nearly didn't make it that time,' he said. 'You'd better stay where you are. They're hanging out of the windows and holding on to the roof down there.'

He nodded towards the carriages in front, and Anna

could see people hanging on to the outsides of the carriages, holding on to anything they could grab hold of. It seemed as if everybody thought that it was going to be the last train out of there for a very long time.

Anna lay gratefully on the floor of the guard's van. Her head was thumping and her throat was sore. Her black woolly stockings had holes in the knees and blood had made smeary, sticky patches where she'd fallen over on the rubble.

Then the sky lit up with searchlights, even before darkness had completely fallen.

'Here they come again,' the guard said, looking as though he'd had enough of it all. 'The sooner this lot's over, the better for all of us. But don't say I said so,' he muttered.

The fireman began to stoke up the boiler and the engine-driver began to make for the safety of the nearest tunnel. The black smoke made Anna's eyes sting. They were moving quickly now, and the tunnel was in sight. One wave of the aircraft passed overhead, dropping a string of bombs, but missing the train. The front part of the train went into the tunnel and the clouds of black smoke grew denser. Anna could hardly breathe as the guard's van was just about to go into the tunnel too. Then the train jolted to a stop. Anna saw a red flash in the blackness of the tunnel ahead. There was a huge explosion that almost deafened her ears; then another; then another. Anna could see red-hot flames in the solid blackness of the tunnel, and the noise was indescribable. She could hear screams and shouts and shrieks coming from the black fiery hole. It was a direct hit on the tunnel, but just ahead of her, she could see a patch of light through the swirling smoke.

Anna crawled and pulled herself towards the small patch of light, hardly able to breathe at all. She dragged herself over the body of the guard. He was dead, almost buried by rocks and stones that had fallen from the tunnel. She pulled herself forward on anything she could get hold of, over the rubble. She could feel the heat behind her and she thought it was going to swallow her up. But then fresh air hit her as she struggled through the small opening, all that was left of the tunnel arch. She rolled over, down the embankment, not knowing where she was any more. Her head was full of heat and noise, and she lay still for a long time. It seemed as if the air-raid was in her own head and all the fire was in her own body.

Anna realized she was lying on her back, looking at the sky. Gradually she realized too that the lights weren't in her head—they were flashes in the sky. And the roaring in her ears was the sound of bombs and anti-aircraft guns. The last wave of bombers passed over and Anna stayed still for a long time.

Stiff and cold and numb, Anna sat up slowly. She had to force herself to stand up. The whole sky was lit up by a smoky red glow, very bright on the skyline where the city was on fire. Anna smoothed down her skirt and saw it was filled with holes which were black at the edges. She took off her coat, slowly and painfully, to inspect it. It was full of burn-holes as well. Then Anna guessed that by rolling down the embankment and finishing up on her back, she had probably saved herself from being burnt, because this had put out the flames.

There was only one thought in her head now. She had to get back to Kati and Nikki. She had good news to tell them, that Father was still alive, in the hospital. She put her coat on again and began to walk towards the main road, which ran almost parallel to the railway line. She had to scramble back up the embankment and cross the line where the tunnel was. Thick black smoke was still coming out of the hole. Even the ground was hot, and there was wreckage everywhere, but Anna couldn't see a single person, alive or dead, because the tunnel had caved in almost along the whole length of the train. She hurried past.

At last Anna got to the road and started to walk. It was only then she realized she hadn't got any shoes on. She kept on walking.

'If I go in this direction,' she thought, 'I'll get there. I've got to keep going. I've got to tell them the news about Father.'

She tried humming marches in her head to keep her feet on the move. She had no idea of the time, except that it was quite dark now, and clouds had dimmed the 'bombers' moon'.

Anna didn't dare to stop or sit down. She kept talking to herself. 'If I sit down, I'll never be able to get up again. I'll just die. Now I've found Father again, I don't want to die. I've got to get back to Kati and Nikki.'

Then she heard the distant hum of an engine. Thinking it might be a stray bomber, she pressed herself into the hedge. But it was a van with an open back, bumping warily along the road, showing no lights because of the blackout.

'Help, help!' Anna shouted, waving her arms about.

The driver's mate flashed a torch briefly towards the hedge. The van stopped.

'Watch that light!' the driver snapped.

'It's a girl,' his mate said in surprise, as Anna cautiously came towards the van.

'Oh yes?' the driver said, suddenly sounding interested. His expression changed as soon as he got a closer look at Anna. She was streaked with soot and blood. The whole of the front of her coat was stiff with the dried blood from the dead guard's body. Anna remembered how she'd had to crawl over him. Her black woolly stockings were in shreds and her feet were poking through big holes.

'God,' the mate said. 'She stinks of blood and bonfires.' He held his nose between his two fingers.

'Please give me a lift,' Anna croaked, her throat still full of soot and smoke. 'I've got to get home. To my little brother and sister. The village isn't that far. Please give me a lift.'

'Get up in the back. We'll drop you off where the road forks. The village isn't far from there,' the driver said. 'She's no beauty,' he muttered to his mate. 'Go on. Get in the back. We don't want all that muck in the front with us.'

Anna climbed stiffly into the open back of the van and sat on the floor, leaning against the cab. The van bumped and bounced, but she didn't even care. She could see the pale grey of the morning beginning to light up the smoky sky, and, although it was very cold, she dozed off.

She was wakened sharply when the van stopped with a jerk.

'Out you get, kid. On your way,' the mate shouted, and he banged his fist on the metal side of the van. 'God,' he said to the driver. 'She looks even worse in the daylight.'

Anna slid painfully down the side of the van and it shot off almost before her feet touched the ground.

Anna looked round. The men had put her off where they said they would, and she knew it wasn't far now. But walking was almost too painful. She could hardly put one foot in front of the other. Suddenly she could feel all the bruises and burns and cuts. She tried a few more steps. Then a few more. Then she sat down in despair by the roadside. It seemed as if her arms and legs didn't belong to her. They were floating away. They wouldn't do anything she wanted them to do. She closed her eyes.

'Hey, what you doing out here? What you done to yourself? Man got you, did he?'

Anna opened her eyes. It was old Frau Schneider with her hand-cart. Frau Schneider had a little farm just outside the village and went out every morning with her hand-cart to collect mushrooms and horse-manure. She was old and dirty and the village children thought she was a witch.

'Please help me. I've been bombed,' Anna said. 'I've got to get back home.'

'Don't look as if you're going to get anywhere. Lost

your shoes, have you?' Frau Schneider sounded quite smug. 'Here. Get in the cart. Spread a sack out there. A bit smelly, but you don't smell too sweet yourself!' She laughed at her little joke.

Anna clambered into the hand-cart and sat on the sacks. Frau Schneider pulled the cart behind her, with her arms wrapped round the two long shafts. Anna had often laughed at the way Frau Schneider pulled her hand-cart, as if she was a horse or a donkey.

'If ever I have a hand-cart,' Anna used to think, 'I'll push it. Not pull it, like a farm animal.' But now she was just thankful for the lift.

While she was sitting in the hand-cart, Anna suddenly thought about George, and what George had said about freedom being the main thing. But who was free? Not George any longer. Not Father. Not Uncle Franz. Even Uncle Hans wasn't really free, because he didn't dare go out of the cellar. Anyway, how could you be really free if there were so many things to be afraid of all the time?

Somewhere in the distance, she heard a fox bark, and a bird began its morning song. 'It's alright for them,' Anna thought. 'They don't even need to think. If you're an animal, you just do things without thinking.'

'Here we are. Out you get.' Frau Schneider was very pleased with herself. She put Anna down right on the doorstep of Grandmother's house. There were people out and about in the street by now, and they looked at Anna in amazement as she crawled out of the hand-cart.

Anna thanked Frau Schneider, who just grunted and

went on her way. Anna hammered on the front door.

'It's me. It's me. Open the door. Hurry up. Come on.'

She saw Kati's dark eyes peering through the crack of the door as it opened. Kati gave a shout of joy and fell on Anna, quickly followed by Nikki. They didn't seem to notice the blood and soot. Even the peculiar smell of Frau Schneider's hand-cart—which was now all over Anna and her clothes—didn't stop them.

'Anni. Anni. We thought you were dead too.' Kati began to cry all over Anna's shoulder. 'Don't go again. Please don't go again.'

Anna forgot all her aches and pains for a moment, and hugged Kati and Nikki.

'I'll never go again,' she promised. 'I'll never leave you, honest. And guess what? Father's alive, in the hospital. We've found Father again.'

CHAPTER

7

'The best thing you can hope for, is that the Americans or the English get to him before the SS start up another Euthanasia Programme to put down people who make a nuisance of themselves. People like him'll be the first to be got rid of, that's a certainty. People's ashes coming home in cardboard boxes again, and no questions asked. That's what they'll be up to next, given the chance.'

This was Karl's response to Anna's great news that Father was alive, and in the Holy Cross Hospital. Anna had thought up lots of wild schemes to rescue him and smuggle him back home, but all the adults said her schemes were quite impossible.

'What a day-dreamer you still are,' Erika said. 'I thought you'd grown out of that. You've got to be more practical.'

Even Uncle Hans agreed with Erika and Karl that all they could do at the moment was to hope for the best. Anna had to accept that there wasn't anything she could do. There were air-raids day and night; the Allied forces were advancing into Germany; the SS and the Gestapo were redoubling their efforts to prop up Hitler's regime; the roads and railways were being shelled and bombed all the time, and floods of refugees were coming in from the east so that travelling was almost impossible. So Anna prayed every night that the Americans or the English would get to Father before the SS did.

Having Uncle Hans in the house was a great help to Anna, though he had to stay out of sight. He fixed things that got broken and even made a new hen-house, although the hens weren't laying very well, because Anna couldn't get the right food for them.

When the winter got very cold, Uncle Hans moved the hens and the new hen-house into the cellar where he was living. He stored Kati's potatoes there as well, because rations were getting short, and people were getting hungry and ready to steal anything they could eat. Like everybody else, Anna used to go round the farms to buy milk and meat and flour. When they ran out of money (because nobody was earning anything, with Father locked up in the hospital and Mother lost in the Münster air-raid), Anna used to take valuable things from the house to barter with. Erika and Karl and Aunt Margarethe helped out, but they were going short as well. Anna had used up all the bottles of wine from Father's cellar doing this, so there was plenty of room down there now.

Then one day, at the end of winter, Uncle Hans and Nikki fell ill with a fever.

'We'll all move down into the cellar,' Anna said. 'It'll

be easier to look after them, if we're all together. And it'll be safer, with all these air-raids. We'll make it as comfortable as we can.'

Anna and Kati dragged their mattresses down into the cellar. They brought down the kitchen table and some stools to sit on among the hens and potatoes. The cellar was lit by the daylight that seeped through the grating under the front step. Karl brought them a pick-axe and a shovel, in case the house got a direct hit and they had to dig their way out. Anna found an old oil-lamp, like the ones they'd used in Stolp, and put it on the table to use at night-time. She had a sheet of blackout material to pull across the grating, so that they didn't break the blackout when she lit the lamp.

Everybody in the village was waiting for the end of the war, at least as far as they were concerned. They were all wondering what would happen to them. Official papers and files were being put on bonfires; then water was poured over the bonfires, so that they wouldn't light up the village at night. There had been no school for weeks and the rumble of guns was heard continuously in the distance.

'The sooner they get here, the better,' Uncle Hans gasped. His fever was worse and he could hardly speak. 'Let's hope it's the Americans or the English that get here first. Not the French. They'll send in the black Moroccans, ahead of all the rest. They always do. Murdering, raping, looting.'

'Is it true they eat babies?' Kati asked fearfully. 'Will they eat us too?'

'Just pray it isn't them,' Uncle Hans muttered. 'They can't be more than ten miles away.'

Anna pulled his greatcoat over him as he shivered with the fever. There was no heating in the cellar.

'I'll go to the farm,' Anna said. 'To get some milk. I should be able to make it there and back again before the next raid. But whatever can I take to sell?'

She looked round at the bare cellar in desperation, and her eyes fell on the photograph of Grandmother in its tarnished old frame. They'd brought it down from the kitchen and put it on the table in the cellar.

'I'll take the photo out,' Anna said. 'I'm sure that frame's silver. It must be worth lots. Maybe I can get a loaf as well.'

Uncle Hans was almost too weak to talk. 'Take care,' he whispered. 'You shouldn't have to do this, Anna, just a girl like you.'

'I'll be all right,' Anna said, taking an enamel jug and a basket in which she put the photo frame. 'If it's true what they say about the dogs, it'll be easier.'

'What about the dogs?' Kati asked, wide-eyed, because the farm dogs were savage Dobermans.

'Erika said somebody stole one and ate it!' Anna replied. 'They must have been very brave. I wouldn't go near one of those dogs.'

'One by one, they'll disappear,' Uncle Hans said. 'You'll see. When people are hungry enough, they get very brave. I saw that in the east.' Then he lapsed into silence with his eyes closed.

Anna stood on the doorstep and looked at the sky. It

was grey and cloudy. She couldn't see any sign of a plane. She knelt down and listened with her ear close to the ground. That way you could hear aircraft long before you could see them. She and Kati used to listen for trains like that, in the old days. You could hear the rumble and feel the vibration long before the trains arrived. Now the air-raids were so heavy, the planes filled the sky like a blanket when they came over, aiming at the big towns and scouring the countryside for the retreating German army. You could hear the planes coming, just like the trains.

It was all quiet, so Anna ran as fast as she could down the street and across the fields to the nearest farm. The farm dogs started barking as she got near. She stood still, out of reach of the chained dogs. There were three Dobermans, snarling and growling, but one heavy chain lay broken on the ground. So it was true. One of the dogs had been stolen for food.

The farm-woman came out and shouted the dogs to silence. Seeing Anna, who had been there often, she asked: 'What d'you want? I'm selling food, not giving it away.'

Anna held up the photo frame. 'It's real silver,' she shouted back. 'It's got the silver mark on it. For some milk and a loaf.'

The farm-woman came for a closer look. She was wearing clogs and several black bunchy skirts down to the ankles. She had lots of different jumpers on, with holes in. Her hair was scraped back from her face and she had a dirty shawl over her head.

Anna held the photo frame out to her, pointing to the

silver mark, but she didn't let go of it, in case the woman just snatched it away and wouldn't give her anything for it.

'Well, if it's the best you can do,' the woman grumbled. 'Come with me. I'm not fetching and carrying for the likes of you.'

She led Anna safely past the dogs, into a shed. There were several milk churns there, and a big wicker basket on the floor with loaves in it. She scooped some milk into Anna's jug and gave her a loaf from the basket, snatching the photo frame from her at the same time. Then she turned away and stumped off, leaving Anna to creep past the snarling dogs.

Anna walked home carefully, so as not to spill the milk. She went safely across the fields to the cobbled village street. She was so busy keeping an eye on the milk that she didn't notice the planes at first. But then she heard a dull roar in the distance, and looked up to see hundreds of American bombers making their way to the Canal. They seemed a safe distance away, so she kept on walking.

Suddenly one of the low-fliers broke away from the rest. It was one of the fighter planes accompanying the bombers. It swooped low towards the village. There was nobody else in sight, and Anna remembered the day when six schoolboys had been gunned down as they ran for the cover of a hedge. Anna couldn't run— her legs wouldn't work. The plane came lower and lower, following the street, towards her. Anna fell on her knees, clutching the loaf and the jug of milk. The noise of the engine deafened her. She looked up and she could see the pilot quite clearly.

Then the plane had gone beyond her. She forced herself to turn her head. The plane was gaining height and, as it did, the pilot dipped his wings to her, and disappeared into the clouds.

Anna was trembling and covered with sweat when she got back to Grandmother's house. She kicked the grating under the step. 'Let me in! Let me in! Hurry up!' she shouted.

Kati unlocked and unbolted the front door, and Anna went straight down into the cellar.

'You clever thing!' Kati shouted, running down after her. 'You got something!'

'You go back and lock up again,' Anna said sharply. '*Then* you can have something.'

Anna put the loaf on the kitchen table and put some of the milk in a pan with water. She lit the little camping stove they used for cooking in the cellar, and put the pan on to boil. She watched it carefully, to make sure it didn't boil over.

'Listen, what's that?' she said suddenly, looking up from the pan.

They all held their breath, listening hard. There was a heavy rumbling sound, louder than planes or trains. Anna peered up through the grating under the front step. She was just in time to see a huge tank, with soldiers and guns all over it, come rolling down the village street. It completely filled the road and nearly scraped the houses.

Anna could see the tank wasn't German, because there weren't any swastikas on it. Then it rumbled out of sight. For a while, it was all quiet again.

'What shall I do? What shall I do?' Anna asked Uncle Hans, shaking him. He didn't answer. His eyes were closed and he seemed unconscious. She could tell he was still alive, by his feverish breathing.

'Listen, listen!' Kati said, clutching Anna's arm. There was a new sound, in the distance, but getting nearer and louder: shouting, screaming, shooting, glass smashing. It came from the direction of the slave-workers' camp.

Anna remembered what Uncle Hans had said, about paying for what was going on there, treating men worse than animals. They'd get their revenge one day.

'Quick!' Anna said to Kati, and she picked up Nikki. 'It's the prisoners at the camp. They've broken out. We've got to hide.' She threw a blanket over Uncle Hans and pushed Kati in front of her upstairs.

'We'll hide like we used to do,' Anna said to Kati. 'In the big wardrobe. Hurry up.'

It was the big mahogany wardrobe in Mother's room. It opened with two great doors, almost like a room itself. At the back was a sliding door, opening into a compartment for cases and boxes. When they'd been little, Anna and Kati had played hide-and-seek in there. One day, the whole wardrobe had toppled over, with them inside it. It had taken Father and Uncle Hans all their strength to lift it up again. Mother said they'd been lucky not to suffocate. After that, Father had bolted the wardrobe to the floor and drilled air holes in the top of the compartment at the back.

Anna pushed aside Mother's dresses that were still

hanging there, and slid open the panel at the back. She propped Nikki up in a corner and said: 'Now let's pretend it's hide-and-seek, Kati. No talking at all.'

She could hear Nikki wheezing, but there was nothing she could do about it.

Kati crouched obediently in one corner, with her knees under her chin, leaning against the wall. Anna pulled the big outer doors together, and closed up the gap in the clothes. Then she squeezed in herself, sliding the panel across and wedging it firm by ramming her shoe under it.

'I want to get out,' Kati wailed. 'It's too dark. I don't want to play.'

'Close your eyes and then open them again,' Anna said. 'Then you'll see little lights in the roof where Father drilled the holes.'

Kati tried this. It was true. She could see spots of light. 'I still don't like it,' she moaned. 'And I'm hungry. You didn't give me any of that loaf.'

'If you're really good, and promise not to make a sound,' Anna hissed at Kati, 'I'll go down and get the loaf. Then you can have something to eat.'

Anna could have kicked herself for leaving the loaf down in the cellar on the table. 'That's me,' she thought. 'Scatter-brains again!'

Anna crept out of the wardrobe, carefully straightening up the clothes and closing the big doors behind her. In the street outside she could hear people running and screaming, windows smashing, shouting and banging.

She ran as fast as she could down all the stairs into the cellar. She reached out to pick up the loaf and the jug of milk. Then, from behind, a claw-like hand grabbed her wrist before she could get hold of the loaf. She felt her throat being crushed by another hand. She looked up, terrified and choking, and saw the face of a man behind her, dirty, haggard, all skin and bones, with wild savage eyes and straggling hair.

The man let go of her wrist and snatched up the bread knife from the table. Anna knew he must be one of the slave-workers from the camp. She was sure he was going to kill her, but while he was waving the knife in front of her face, nearer and nearer, and choking her more and more, another figure jumped on him from the cellar steps, hitting him on the back of the head with one of the stools. The knife dropped and the man fell to the ground. Anna could see blood on the stool and on the floor, but she was too frightened to move and stood staring at the man who'd saved her life. Green eyes and high cheek bones . . . a look of recognition passed between them.

'Hide,' the man said, in German. 'Hide. Until the Allies come. It's not safe anywhere. The prisoners from the camp are running wild.'

He picked the bread knife up off the floor and took the loaf off the table. Anna was just standing there, rubbing her throat, unable to say anything. After a brief hesitation, the man made the sign of the cross on the bottom of the loaf with the knife, and handed the loaf to Anna.

'Go, Anna,' he said. 'Go now. Hide.' Then he went quickly up the cellar steps and out of the house, dragging the unconscious man behind him.

Anna forced herself to move. She ran back upstairs with the loaf. 'It was George,' she was thinking frantically. 'He remembered me. He said my name.'

Inside the cubby-hole again, with all the doors closed, she broke bits off the loaf and shared it with Kati. Nikki was too ill to eat. He was sitting slumped in his corner with his eyes closed.

'It's too dry,' Kati complained. 'I'm thirsty.'

'Well, I'm not going out there again to get you a drink. Hush! I can hear something—footsteps—,' Anna whispered back.

They crouched in the dark and listened to the sound of heavy feet pounding up the stairs. Doors banged. There was the sound of glass smashing, furniture being toppled over, banging and shouting. They sat in terrified silence as they heard the big doors of the wardrobe being flung open. They could hear the clothes being swished on the rails and loud voices, shouting and laughing. It was a language the children didn't understand, but the escaped men didn't guess there was a compartment at the back of the wardrobe, and mother's old clothes didn't interest them.

After a while the footsteps went away again, and all the noise in the room died down. The children sat there in the silent, stifling darkness. Anna guessed that the men had gone off to find a house with better things in it. She knew there was nothing valuable left in Grandmother's house, because she had used up everything that was worth anything to buy food during the past few weeks. But they stayed there in the little black hole because they were afraid to move.

CHAPTER

8

Anna heard heavy footsteps again. It had been quiet for a long time. More than one day, perhaps more than two. Anna couldn't tell. All the bread had gone and she and Kati had sucked their fingers because they were so thirsty. Nikki was in a silent heap and Anna wondered if he was dead. She couldn't hear him wheezing any more.

Anna could hear the footsteps in the bedroom now, quite close at hand. Had the escaped men come back? The wardrobe doors were opened and Anna heard the clothes being swished about on the rails.

There were voices. Not shouting. Talking. And not German. Anna listened intently. Was it English? She'd learnt quite a lot of English at school. What language was it?

'Nothing doing. They've been and gone, poor devils. Let's get out of here,' a voice was saying.

It was English; Anna could recognize most of the words, but it wasn't school English. Was it American? Were the Americans here?

Anna couldn't stand it any longer. 'Help, help!' she croaked.

'Who's there?' came a sharp reply in English. 'Hands up! Come out with your hands up—or I'll shoot!'

'Not to shoot, please, not to shoot,' Anna shouted, trying to remember the words she'd learnt in the English lessons. The words didn't want to come into her head. 'Not to shoot, please. Here is only children!'

Anna slid the panel across and crawled out of the wardrobe, between Mother's dresses, blinking in the bright daylight. She tried to pull Kati out behind her, but she was too weak. As her screwed-up eyes got used to the daylight, she saw she was looking straight at two rifles, pointing right at her face.

'Christ!' one of the soldiers said, lowering his gun. 'Kids! Phew!' And he turned his head away from the stink of the cubby-hole where they'd been hiding for two days. 'Let's get some fresh air.'

But all the same he put out his hand to help Anna and Kati crawl out of the wardrobe.

Kati screamed hoarsely when her eyes focused in the unaccustomed light. 'It's the Moroccans. They'll eat us.'

'What she say?' asked one of the black American soldiers.

Anna had never seen a black man before, but she knew these were not Moroccans, because Moroccans spoke French, not English. She knew the name of only one black American—Jesse Owens. Father had always been very pleased that the black runner had made Hitler furious by winning lots of gold medals in the Berlin Olympic Games.

'Jesse Owens number one,' Anna said desperately, in English.

The man looked at her in amazement, then he smiled. 'Hey, kid. You speak English good. What's up here? You kids Jews or something, hiding from the Krauts?' he asked. 'How long you been in that stink-hole? You sure don't smell so good. Red Cross'll be coming through before long. They'll look after you.'

Kati was pulling at Anna's arm. 'Are they going to eat us?' she asked. 'Is it still the same war?'

'What she say, kid?' the black soldier asked again.

Anna translated into English: 'She said, "Is it still the same war?"'

'The same war?' he repeated. 'Well, I guess it's the same war. It's the only war I know of at the moment! But it's all over for you kids now. Red Cross'll be here soon,' he said again, as if he didn't quite know what to do about them.

The other soldier had lifted Nikki out of the wardrobe. He was all floppy, like a rag-doll. 'He's in a bad way,' he said. 'Needs a doctor.'

He put Nikki down on the bed. 'Can't you call a doctor, or something?' he asked Anna. 'Anybody else in the house?'

'There's no doctors left in the village,' Anna said. 'They've all been called up. And there's only us and Uncle Hans, and I think he's dead.'

'You'd better show us,' the soldiers said.

Kati crawled up on the bed and lay down next to Nikki because she felt too weak to do anything. Anna thought they looked more dirty and ragged than any gypsy children she'd ever seen. Kati didn't look like a 'little doughnut' anymore, she was so thin and pale. Anna knew she must look the same. She scarcely had the strength to lead the soldiers down into the cellar, but she wanted to get out of the bedroom as quickly as possible, because it had been completely wrecked by the escaped prisoners. The windows were broken; all the drawers had been pulled out; clothes and hairbrushes and shoes were scattered everywhere. The big mirror had been smashed and the dainty bedroom chairs were in pieces. Anna didn't want to see it.

When they got into the cellar, Anna could see the pool of blood where the man who'd attacked her had fallen, when George hit him with the stool. The soldiers took no notice of it however.

One of the soldiers spat at the sight of Uncle Hans' German army greatcoat, but when they saw his medical orderly's badge, they were more friendly and took a quick look at him.

'Well, he's not dead yet,' one of them said cheerfully. 'Needs a doctor. Wait for the Red Cross.'

Anna had turned on the little water tap in the cellar and was drinking from it furiously. She looked for the enamel milk jug, to take some water to Kati and Nikki. It had been knocked on the floor and stamped on, but she managed to fill it with water. Looking round, Anna could see that the whole house had been wrecked. The escaped men must have torn it apart. Anna guessed that Uncle Hans had been lucky—very lucky. Either they hadn't seen him under the blanket because it was so dim in the cellar; or they'd thought he was dead already. He certainly looked it.

The few hens they still had down there had dis-appeared and so had all the potatoes they were carefully hoarding. The hen-house had been broken to pieces.

'Hey, kid,' one of the soldiers said to Anna. 'Get yourself cleaned up and report to our HQ. They need an interpreter down there. I'll write out a pass for you.'

He wrote something on a piece of paper, and was going to hand it to Anna. Then he seemed to notice again how dirty and smelly and untidy she was, and he put it down on the wooden table for her to pick up instead. Then the two soldiers left, and Anna never saw them again.

Anna poured some water down Uncle Hans' mouth and took some up to Kati and Nikki. Then she sat on the bed beside them, looking in despair at all the wreckage.

'How long will it be before the Red Cross gets here?' she wondered. 'Is the war really over? Maybe the Red Cross will get Father back—'

Outside in the street she could hear shots being fired, and shouting and running footsteps. Standing well back, she looked through the broken window of the bedroom. All the houses had broken windows, some had the doors hacked down, and the street was full of glass and all sorts of stuff that the escaped prisoners had thrown out of the houses—broken furniture, dresses, shoes, coats, broken cups and saucers. She could see three dead bodies in the road and she knew from their ragged clothes that they were from the slave-labour camp. But she could tell George wasn't one of them. It reminded Anna of market day, because people were rushing in and out of the houses picking up what they could find in the street—clothes, pots, chairs, anything. They dodged between the American jeeps and armoured cars and took no notice of the soldiers on foot, even though they had their rifles at the ready, looking out for snipers. Nobody in the village was interested in sniping; mostly they were very glad that it was the Americans who had got there first. Everybody already knew that Americans had food and cigarettes.

Then Anna saw a group of soldiers dragging people out of one of the houses, and hitting them with the butt-end of their rifles. She pulled Kati off the bed.

'Come on,' she said to Kati. 'Help me get Nikki downstairs. We'll have to live in the cellar again. The whole house is wrecked and it's the only place we'll be safe.'

'If the war's over, why isn't it all nice again, like before?' Kati asked, beginning to grizzle. Anna felt she couldn't begin to answer that question, so she didn't even try.

'Come on,' she said sternly. 'Stop moaning. Try to make yourself useful and help me with Nikki.' She heard herself with surprise. It sounded just like Mother talking.

Even though Nikki was so thin and light, it was slow work getting him downstairs into the cellar.

'My head's all muzzy,' Kati moaned. 'I can't see properly. There's lots of dots in front of my eyes.'

They came down one stair at a time, sitting down,

but at last they got into the cellar and Anna bolted the door.

'Isn't there anything to eat anywhere?' Kati asked desperately.

'All we've got at the moment is water,' Anna said, and she gave Kati a drink from an enamel beaker that she'd found on the floor. She noticed the pass on the table. 'When it's all gone quiet again, I'll go and find the American HQ, but we'll all have to get cleaned up first,' Anna said, and set about filling the sink with water.

There was a loud banging at the cellar door. 'Let us in! Quick! It's Erika and Karl.'

Anna unbolted the door, and Erika and Karl came in, carrying two huge cans. 'Lock up again. Quick!' Erika said. 'We came to see how you were. After those terrible Poles! There's been rape and murder in the village. We hid in the loft. Poor Karl. I had to pull him up the ladder. Are you all right? I can see you are—and look here—' she put the two huge cans on the table— 'Sausages—enough for a month!'

'Wherever did they come from?' Anna asked, giving the can-opener to Erika, and looking in amazement at the cans. They were as big as the food cans in the convent kitchen, which had to do meals for about a hundred people.

'Don't ask! But I'll tell you this much. An American supply truck overturned—hit a shell-hole in the road. You never saw such a rush. Like ants going for the honey. One minute, hundreds of cans of food in the road. The next minute, nothing, and not a soul in sight, either.'

Erika pulled off the lid and Anna sniffed the air. 'What a lovely smell,' she said.

'Right!' agreed Karl. 'You could say that these Yankee sausages have saved our bacon!'

Erika showed Anna how to heat up the jelly in the can and give it to Uncle Hans and Nikki, because they were too weak to eat the sausages. The smell of the hot sausages cheered everybody up.

Anna was wondering what had happened to George, but she knew it was no use saying anything to Erika and Karl on that subject, so she told them about the pass instead, and about being an interpreter.

Erika was delighted and full of plans about what Anna could do—and get—if she worked at the HQ. She helped to get Anna smartened up, and sent her off as soon as the streets seemed safe, to find the HQ.

CHAPTER

9

'Next!' the officer shouted, and he pushed another pile of forms in front of Anna. They were sitting side by side at a huge desk in the gymnasium of the Convent High School. This was the American HQ and Anna recognized the desk—it was the one Mother Superior used to have in her office. The gymnasium was full of people waiting to register and fill up the forms and be 'de-Nazified'. There were hardly any chairs, so they were either standing or sitting on the floor. There were old men and women, and young women and children. There were no young men left in the village, because they had all been forced to join the 'werewolves' in Hitler's last desperate attempt to hold back the Allied advance. As there were 133 questions to be answered, it all took a long time. The next person came and sat in the chair facing the officer, waiting to be questioned. It was going to be another long, tiring day, Anna's third day at the HQ.

During the break for lunch, the officer brought her a sandwich and some coffee. His name was Captain

Roberts and he was always very kind and polite to Anna. He had a desk job because he'd been injured in the Battle of the Bulge. Anna often wondered about George, and now she got her courage together to ask.

'What happened to the foreign workers? From the labour camp?' Anna asked Captain Roberts, hesitantly, because she remembered the three dead men she'd seen from the broken window in the bedroom at Grandmother's house.

'From that hell-hole just outside the village?' Captain Roberts answered. 'Those poor devils. Some of 'em got shot, when we first occupied the place. Running wild, madmen, they were. Looting, murdering, raping.'

'But who shot them?' Anna asked.

'We did,' the American said shortly. 'To restore order. You got to have law and order.'

'But . . .' Anna wasn't sure what to say next, except that it didn't seem fair.

'Don't "but" me,' the American replied, and he sounded angry. 'I don't like it. You don't like it. Nobody don't like it. Poor devils—like skeletons, they were. But you got to have law and order.'

Anna wondered if she dared ask any more questions, but he seemed to read her mind.

'There's a list of identified dead,' he said, rummaging in the drawers of the desk. He pulled out a file. 'Let's look in here. Anybody you know?' He handed a sheaf of papers to Anna.

Anna looked through the list of names. They all seemed to end in -*ski* or -*ov*, but the name Kempinski wasn't there.

'What happened to all the others?' Anna asked, handing back the file.

'There's a camp for displaced persons, a few miles away. Maybe some are there. Mostly those camps are full of refugees coming in from the east, though. They're probably living rough. Hiding.'

'Why are all these people coming here from the east?' Anna asked, remembering Stolp and Pastor Schmidt and his wife.

'To get away from the Russians, that's why,' Captain Roberts replied. Anna remembered Father's warning, written on the back of a Christmas card, telling them to come back to the west, after the German defeat at Stalingrad. She wondered how Father had known what was going to happen. If they hadn't left Stolp then, they would be refugees too, displaced persons living in a camp, or prisoners of the Russians. It was thanks to Father that they still had Grandmother's house to live in and she'd got this job with the Americans. The Red Cross still hadn't sent them any word about Father, but that wasn't surprising, since prisoners of war were being counted in hundreds of thousands. Anna hadn't given up hope.

Captain Roberts was still talking about the foreign workers. 'Some of them just disappeared,' he said. 'But they'll be caught—no papers—no identity cards—no passports. Stateless, that's what they are. Nobody'll want to go back to the east, not with the Reds running things. There'll be too many scores to settle. It'll be Siberia for most of them. And that's if they're lucky.'

Then the afternoon session started, and Anna translated the answers to the 133 questions that each person over the age of eighteen had to answer.

'It's amazing,' the American said sarcastically to Anna, as the questions were being answered. 'We don't seem to have a single Party Member in the whole village! Makes you wonder who did support Hitler! Anyway, we'll soon see—there's a complete list of Party Members been found in Munich. As soon as we get a copy of that, we'll weed 'em out.'

Anna just nodded. She knew who was lying and who wasn't. She didn't say anything, but she decided to warn Karl and Erika about the list, because they'd both been Party Members. As far as she knew, they hadn't actually done anything wrong. Karl had been a soldier, but it seemed to Anna that it wasn't ordinary soldiers that the Americans were after. And he'd said Hitler had the right way with the Jews—but he hadn't actually done anything. At least, she didn't think so. Nothing really bad. Nothing very good either, when she came to think of it. Mostly it was Erika who'd helped them, with Aunt Margarethe.

At the end of the afternoon session, when Captain Roberts had gone to get some coffee, Anna acted almost without thinking. She used the office telephone to ring the Commander-in-Charge of the displaced persons camp, and enquire whether he had a George Kempinski on his list. She made her voice sound very official. The answer was 'No', and Anna had put down the telephone before Captain Roberts came back with the coffee. She wondered how she'd dared to do it—and now she didn't know what to do next about George.

Perhaps she would never find out what had happened to him.

Captain Roberts gave Anna a lift home in the jeep, and gave her a package as she got out. She thanked him—she knew what was in it—bread, milk powder, cans of sausages and ham, and medicine for Nikki. He was always so kind and generous that Anna felt even worse about not telling him who was lying on the forms, and not asking if she could use the phone. Kati came running out to her.

'Come and see what I've got!' she said, dragging Anna into the courtyard at the back. There were three hens, scratching in the dirt.

'Wherever did you get those from?' Anna asked, irritated.

'They were lost and I found them,' Kati answered.

'I think that's stealing,' Anna said.

'No it isn't. They didn't have anywhere to go. They like it here,' Kati answered. 'They might lay eggs, if we can feed them right.'

'Uncle Hans'll have to sit and guard them,' Anna said. 'They'll be stolen before tomorrow, if you don't watch out.'

The schools were still closed and so were all the shops. There was no food, except what the Red Cross and the Quakers brought in food parcels, and what people could beg or steal off the Americans. Only the farmers had food, and they were asking such high prices that many people couldn't raise the money. Anna knew that they were luckier than most people, because of her job at the HQ.

Then one day the war was really over. It was 8 May 1945, and it was official. At the HQ the American soldiers were all cheering and shouting and drinking beer out of cans. Then Anna heard shots being fired. Captain Roberts got up from the desk to see what was going on outside.

At the back of the PX canteen a group of drunken American soldiers were firing their rifles in the air and beating up a man who looked like a bundle of rags. When they saw Captain Roberts, they quietened down, hanging on to their prisoner.

'What's going on here?' Captain Roberts demanded.

'A Red stealing from the PX stores,' they said.

Anna had come out to see what was happening. Then she rushed forwards. 'It's my brother,' she shouted. 'That's my brother.'

Captain Roberts ordered the soldiers to let go of the man. 'I thought your brother was ten years old,' he said, looking suspicious.

'It's another one, one I didn't tell you about,' Anna said. 'He's been missing. Like my Father.' Anna grabbed George's wrist, and it was like holding a drumstick.

Because it was George that the soldiers were holding—George—so bony and dirty that Anna hardly recognized him. But his green eyes looked at her in recognition.

Captain Roberts waved the soldiers on their way, and they went off to continue their celebration of VE day. 'I see,' the captain said. 'Well, keep this newly-found brother of yours out of my way, or I might just find out that he's got no papers; that he's a stateless person; and that his name's George Kempinski. And what's more, young woman, all outgoing telephone calls—even to Commanders of displaced persons camps—are monitored. You owe the US Army the price of one telephone call. The war's over now, and I'm going to celebrate. Take my advice, and get him off the streets.'

Captain Roberts turned his back on them and went into the HQ. Anna took George back home with her as fast as possible, and told Uncle Hans all about him. George disappeared to get cleaned up. When he came back into the kitchen, they all looked round at him with surprise. He was clean and tidy again, and half-buried in an old suit of Father's because he was so thin.

'You've got this place nicely tidied up,' he said, with a little smile. 'Better than when I last saw it—just after we'd broken out of the camp.'

Kati had been looking at George full of fear, until he spoke. Then she shouted, 'I know who you are. You're George K. Kempinski from Stolp. You look awful, like a skeleton.' Nikki had been looking alarmed too.

Anna came to George's defence at once. 'We looked just as bad, before the Americans came. Hiding in the wardrobe.' But Kati and Nikki didn't want to remember the bad days, and they closed in on George with lots of questions, while Anna tried to explain what had happened to them.

'It's because Captain Roberts has been so good to us,' Anna said, feeling guilty again. 'He got medicines for Nikki and Uncle Hans, and he gives us food and things.'

'I did a lot of the fixing,' Nikki said. 'I mended chairs and I put glass in the windows. Uncle Hans told me what to do. Uncle Karl told me too. He's good at telling people what to do.'

'Never mind about us,' Anna said. 'What happened to you? I didn't give you away. Somebody must have. But it wasn't me.'

'Anna, Anna, I know you didn't,' George said, slowly chewing the bread and sausage. 'Nothing that happened was your fault.'

'Why d'you eat so slowly?' Nikki asked, curiously, watching George chewing the bread.

'If you eat too much and too quickly after you've been starving, you can die,' George said. 'It was my own fault, really. I was too cocky. I was a fool to carry that picture—the Black Madonna—for a start. Some of those country clowns found it. Then word got round. Then the police came with questions. Pastor Schmidt got put in prison for not handing me over. I didn't think he knew anything when I was at the school, but of course he did. That was why it was so long before they caught up with me, because he kept quiet about me. My own family were all killed in Poland, in the attack on Warsaw in 1939, but I'd been on holiday, at the Baltic Sea. That's where I met Pastor Schmidt. He found me a family to live with, out there near Stolp. I told him I was an orphan. That part was true, of course. But I didn't say I was Polish. Some German families in Poland had the same name, Kempinski.' He smiled and crumbled up some of the bread in his skinny fingers, eating it crumb by crumb. 'Made a great drama of it, didn't I? All that business with K for Kosciuszko! It was all a game then.'

'But you haven't changed your mind, have you?' Anna was full of anxiety. 'You were right. I'm sure you were right. Freedom *is* the most important thing. You do have to be strong against your enemies.'

'No,' George said, thinking hard about it. 'I haven't really changed my mind. But you were right too, Anna. I remember the question you asked: "Who is your enemy?" Now that's a very good question, not easy to answer. I was my own enemy. If I'd been more cautious I mightn't have been caught. And I was Pastor Schmidt's enemy too. It was my fault he got put in prison.'

'I'm sure that's not right,' Anna said. 'Pastor Schmidt wouldn't say that. He did what he wanted to, what he thought was right. If more people had done that, then perhaps this war wouldn't have happened.'

Anna was quite surprised to hear herself arguing with George. Back in the old days, in Stolp, she never argued with him, because he seemed to be so much cleverer than she was, and he knew more. Now it didn't seem like that at all.

George looked surprised too, but he didn't argue. 'Then it was the transit camp. Most of them were booted into trucks and sent out east. God knows where. Because I was young and strong, it was forced labour for me. As you know. I couldn't believe it was you, Anna, the other side of that hedge!'

Anna smiled. 'But I told you where I lived, where Grandmother's house was, when we were in Stolp,' she said.

'All I knew was that I was in a labour-camp in the middle of a field, somewhere in Westphalia. Until we broke out, that is. Then I saw the village's name. It must have been fate!' George said, smiling and picking up the remains of the loaf. He broke a piece off and gave it to her. Anna ate it slowly, thinking over what had happened in just a few years. She told him about Father, Mother and Uncle Franz; and Uncle Hans told his story too.

'You'll have to hide in the cellar, like Uncle Hans did,' Kati said. 'Do we have to bandage him up too, Anna?' she asked.

George looked alarmed, until Kati explained how they'd disguised Uncle Hans. 'Well, thank God we don't have to worry about the Gestapo and the SS any more. I'll be quite happy to stay in the cellar—but without the bandages and the chicken's blood, please.' George almost laughed. 'I've been hiding in sheds and bombed-out buildings since the breakout. Nobody's going to send me back east. I'd rather die.'

'That's what Captain Roberts said would happen—all the Poles would be sent back east,' Anna said, and she turned to Uncle Hans. 'What about Erika and Karl? Will they give George away? To the Americans?'

'There's one way of making sure that Erika and Karl don't do anything you don't want them to do,' Uncle Hans said, with a little smile. 'They were both Party Members, and they won't want anything stirred up. They'll keep quiet about George, and we'll keep quiet about one or two things they don't want to get around to the ears of the de-Nazification court.'

Anna remembered what Karl had said a long time ago, about Hitler having the right way with the Jews. Yet, after Mother died, Erika had been so kind to them.

'That's something I can't understand,' she said to Uncle Hans. 'People are so complicated.'

'That's why it's hard to know who your enemies are,' George said.

'Well, the war's over now. I'm sure things will get better,' Anna said.

'But George has still got to hide,' Nikki said. 'Why does he have to hide if the war's over?'

'Nothing's that simple,' George said, with a grim smile. 'If I haven't got any papers, I'm not supposed to exist!'

'Will you have to live in the cellar for ever?' Kati asked.

'Not if I can help it,' George said. 'One day I'll make a break for it—stow away on a Swedish ship. Sweden's a good place to make for. A neutral country, a democracy. That's what I want. Somewhere where people are really free.'

'But we've only just found you again!' Anna said. She didn't like that idea at all.

'He'll have to do what he thinks is right,' Uncle Hans said, and they left it at that.

CHAPTER

10

'Wait a minute. Brunner. That's your name, isn't it Anna?' Captain Roberts was working his way through a big sheaf of papers. There were long lists of names of Party Members who all had to be de-Nazified, and a much shorter list of people who hadn't been Party Members, who didn't have to be de-Nazified and could be appointed to open the school and run things again in the village.

'Yes,' Anna said, looking up from the pile of forms she was sorting out, hardly daring to hope for good news.

'Officer in the *Luftwaffe*? Your father, d'you think?' He showed Anna the name on his list. Anna could see the paper shaking in her hand because she couldn't stop trembling. But it really was true. It was Father's name on a list of POWs to be sent home for medical reasons. As her father wasn't a Party Member, he was going to be one of the first to come home.

'Funny, that,' the captain said. 'Don't often come across an officer who's not a Party Member.' Anna told him how Father had served in the First World War, and got his commission in the old Flying Corps.

'Flew with the old Red Baron, did he?' Captain Roberts asked with interest, but Anna didn't know what he was talking about. She wanted to rush straight back to Grandmother's house to tell Kati and Nikki the good news. She was just going to ask permission to go when an American officer, whose face she didn't know, came into the gymnasium with one of the officers who was billeted in the village.

'Here's somebody who can maybe help you,' the officer from the village said, and he pointed to Anna. Anna was irritated. She wanted to get off home as soon as possible. But the American went on talking to her.

'Anna, this is Lieutenant Grauberg. He's got a few questions he'd like to ask. See what you can do to help him.'

He pronounced the name 'Grorburg'. The new officer smiled and said: 'Lieutenant Grauberg,' and he used the pronunciation of the region.

Anna was puzzled and forgot her irritation. Americans didn't usually speak German, or use the local pronunciation. That was why they were so glad of her to do this job.

'What would you like to know?' she asked, her English already tinged with an American accent, because she'd been working at the HQ so long.

'Well, you look a bit young to remember what I want to ask about,' he said, in English.

'I'm nearly seventeen,' Anna said, rather haughtily. 'And I've got a very good memory.'

'Does the name "Grauberg" mean anything to you, then?' he asked, again using the pronunciation of the region, although he wasn't speaking in German. Anna suddenly felt cold and full of apprehension. She wished she hadn't boasted about having a good memory. She ought to think before she said anything! That was a habit she'd almost got out of—except that she was careful never to talk about George, who was still living in the cellar, three weeks after she'd found him again on the day the war ended.

This was something she didn't want to remember— the night the Jews were taken. The night before they'd had to leave for Stolp, in the autumn, four years ago. Was it really only four years ago? It seemed like a memory of a different life. The picture of the white nightdress, spread out like snow on the bushes, came into her mind.

Lieutenant Grauberg had seen that expression on people's faces before, when he'd asked questions that people didn't like to be asked. These were things people would rather forget about, from fear or shame.

'OK. Sure,' he said. 'I'll enquire somewhere else.'

'No,' Anna said quickly, making up her mind to speak out. 'You don't need to do that.' And she told him of the events of that day, back in the autumn of 1941. It seemed a long time ago.

Lieutenant Grauberg listened without interrupting. When she stopped talking, he said: 'Would you show me the house? I'm Joseph Grauberg. I left Germany in 1933. My parents sent me to America and I'm a US citizen now. Herr Grauberg was my father.'

Anna noticed that he'd said 'Herr Grauberg', not just 'Grauberg', and she resolved to do the same in future. It wasn't just that it was more respectful, but it made him sound like a real person. That made Anna feel even worse about what had happened.

Anna sat beside Lieutenant Grauberg in the jeep, and directed him to the little side road where the broken-down houses had been. The side road was all over-grown now, and bushes and brambles flapped along the sides of the jeep. Nobody came this way any more, and it was clear that nobody had been there for a very long time. Then they saw the houses—or what was left of them. The old roofs had fallen in and Anna could see the summer swallows diving between the rafters. The crumbling walls were green with ivy and the sun shone through the glassless windows. The bark of the silver birches glinted in the sunlight.

'Nothing,' Lieutenant Grauberg said in a quiet voice. 'Nothing at all. Well, I suppose that's it. I don't know what I thought I'd find. I can hardly remember the place at all. This wasn't where we used to live, not where I lived. No right to feel disappointed. I shouldn't have come back here at all. Should have stayed with my own unit, but I had a few days furlough, and I thought I'd come here—just on the off chance . . .,' and his voice faded away.

'Well, there was something . . .' Anna began to speak, and straightaway she wished she hadn't.

'Something?' he asked sharply. 'What?'

Anna told him about the violin case in the ditch, under the silver birch tree.

'But I expect it's been stolen by now, or rotted away,' she said.

'Doesn't look as if too many people've been down here,' Lieutenant Grauberg said. Anna had to agree with him. The roadway was overgrown and the ditch was filled up. There was an air of desolation about the place and Anna shivered, in spite of the warm sunshine. She thought it was a place that felt haunted, fit for ghosts.

'This must be the tree,' she said, trying to be very factual and down-to-earth. She poked the silver birch with her foot. 'Of course, it's bigger now. And the ditch has filled up.'

Lieutenant Grauberg was crouching down, digging at the base of the tree with his hands. It was quite soft where the ditch had been, and he threw out handfuls of dead leaves and damp peat and tangled roots. He gave a shout: 'There's something here. Come on. Lend a hand.' And Anna began to fling out grass and leaves and soil as well. Lieutenant Grauberg heaved and pulled, and at last the violin case came out of the damp peat. The leather covering of the box was black and peeling, like sunburnt skin. He hugged it to his chest.

'Well, aren't you going to open it?' Anna asked, curious to see if there was anything inside. She wasn't expecting very much. Lieutenant Grauberg put the case on the ground and knelt beside it. Very carefully he prised the lid open with his penknife. He laid the lid wide open. Inside the case was the violin, in perfect condition: it had been protected by the leather-covered case and preserved by the peat in the ditch.

Anna and the lieutenant looked at the violin. At last he said: 'Well, that is something. That is really something.'

They got back into the jeep and Anna carefully held the damp, shabby violin case on her knee. She couldn't understand how the perfect violin could have been preserved in such a tatty-looking case.

Lieutenant Grauberg drove Anna back to Grandmother's house and pulled up outside it.

'Maybe I'll be able to do something for you, one day. Don't forget the name: Joe Grauberg, Lieutenant; US 15th Army.'

Anna thought it wasn't a name she was likely to forget in a hurry, and she was just getting out of the jeep, carefully putting the precious violin in the place where she'd been sitting, when she got an idea.

'Well, as a matter of fact,' she said. 'There is something.' And she told him about George, hiding in the cellar, a stateless person with no papers, who would rather die than go back to the east.

Back in the kitchen at Grandmother's house, Lieutenant Grauberg was sitting at the table, the precious violin in front of him, with Anna, George, and Uncle Hans. Kati and Nikki weren't interested, so they'd gone into the courtyard to feed the hens.

'With American dollars and cigarettes, you can buy anything,' Lieutenant Grauberg was saying. 'George will have to come with me to Düsseldorf. I've got a contact there. We can get him fixed up with papers and a bit of money. Then he's on his own again. I don't want to be court-martialled. Not a word of this is to get out, or it's all off, and he's on the first shipment to the east.'

So George left the village in Lieutenant Grauberg's jeep, and Anna at last had a chance to tell them all the good news about Father and how he was going to be allowed home quite soon. Anna was sad to say goodbye to George again, but at least she felt he was safe with Lieutenant Grauberg, and she didn't doubt at all that the lieutenant really meant what he said. That meant that George would soon be on his way to somewhere safe. Even if she didn't know where it was, Anna felt happier.

'We'll have to get the house all nice for Father,' she said. 'No broken windows: all clean and sparkling.' And she began to get everybody organized for the great day when Father would come back at last. It was summer again.

CHAPTER

11

'I can't imagine what my Karl ever saw in that dreadful Hitler,' Erika was saying. 'Look what he did to your family—all good Germans too—never mind anybody else!'

She was leaning with her elbow on the table in the kitchen of Grandmother's house, with a glass of wine in her other hand. She had to put one elbow on the table because it was so crowded. They were all there, elbow to elbow, round the kitchen table—Father, Anna, Kati, Nikki, Uncle Hans, Uncle Franz, Aunt Margarethe, Maria, Kurt, and Erika and Karl. There was bread and sausage and wine on the table.

'And I've got my Kurt back!' Aunt Margarethe almost beamed. 'Only sixteen he was, when they marched him away. Werewolves! Children, they were. Well, thank God for the Americans—they sent him straight back home to his mother, where he belonged!'

'I think we can drink to that,' Father said, and raised his glass. 'Without them, there'd be no food or drink on this table; and some of us wouldn't be here. But first, we drink to Mother.'

They rose in silence and raised their glasses.'To Mother,' they said, and sat down again.

'And poor Franz,' Erika kept on. 'All those months in that terrible place—.'

'Those bad times are past, thank God!' Uncle Franz answered. 'I can forgive almost everything—but not when you start playing that cello!' He turned to Father, with a smile. 'Haven't we all been through enough torment?'

'How can you hear it if I play in the cellar?' Father asked. 'It's part of my rehabilitation programme!'

'We'll all need rehabilitation if you keep that up!' Uncle Franz was joking.

'How can you joke?' Erika asked. 'Look at you both. So pale and thin. Franz with his glasses and stick. You with your cello! How can you joke?'

'Well, we must look forwards, not backwards,' Uncle Franz said.

'What I can't understand,' Anna turned to Uncle Franz, 'is, how did it all happen? All the things the Nazis did, I mean. Why did the other people let it happen? Why didn't they stop it? Everybody in the village knew when the Jews were going to be taken, but nobody did anything about it. They were all talking about it at school, so everybody knew.'

'I don't think there's a simple answer to all those questions,' Uncle Franz said slowly, peering over the top of his glasses. Anna remembered that he'd never had to wear glasses or walk with a stick before he'd been taken to Dachau. 'But even if you can't find a simple answer, the important thing is to keep on asking the questions. If there's one thing the Devil himself hates, it's people who keep on asking questions like that. Loud and clear. Keep on asking awkward questions.'

Anna put her hand in the pocket of her skirt and ran her fingers over the postcard that had arrived a few days before. It was stamped and franked all over, but there were only three words on it. It read: 'Arrived US. George.'

'What about George, Uncle Franz?' Anna asked. During the past week, since Uncle Franz had arrived back from the American hospital near Munich, Anna had told him all about George and the events of the past two years, since he had been taken to Dachau. 'Will he be safe now?'

'I'm sure he will. Nothing can hold him back now,' Uncle Franz answered.

'The "land of the free and the home of the brave",' Anna said. 'I've learned the words of "The Star Spangled Banner".' Anna was still working as an interpreter. When things got back to normal, she was going to study singing again. 'That would just suit George, wouldn't it? If it's really true. D'you think it's really true, Uncle?'

'It's as near as we're likely to get, I should think,' Uncle Franz said.

'D'you think we'll ever see him again?' Anna asked, feeling sad.

Uncle Franz smiled at her and peered over the top of

his glasses. 'My dear, dear, Anna,' he said. 'That is one thing I'm very sure about. George will be back here again one day. Believe me.'

Anna did believe him, and smiled.